From the MISTS *of* TIME

ANTHONY JOHN DAVIS

Ordering Information:

Prime Seven Media
518 Landmann St.
Tomah City, WI 54660

Printed in the United States of America

Foreword

This is a novel that has its roots in real events that affected real people. The principal protagonists are fictitious, although their personalities, characteristics, and some of their exploits have elements drawn from the lives of people known to and by the author. Others were very real and have been included under aliases.

8 EFTS, 22 EFTS, 43 OTU and 'D' Flight were real flying training units that served with honour throughout the years of the 2nd World War. 659 AOP Squadron RAF was an active service Squadron operating in Normandy with the 21st Army Group, as was the 2nd Northamptonshire Yeomanry, their records were exemplary. The events described in this work of fiction cannot be attributed to any serving Soldier or Airman at any time in the life of these units. I am grateful to all who have provided me with advice and technical detail in my attempt to render the story as true to life as possible. I am particularly grateful to the staff of the Army Air Corps Museum at Middle Wallop, Hampshire, England for their assistance in respect of real events and technical matters regarding operational flying and the control of artillery from an AOP Platform.

The story is written as a tribute to the young men who fought against the tyranny of Nazism in the nineteen thirties and forties, especially those who saw action in the several invasions of the European mainland but especially those who participated in the Liberation of France following Operation Overlord on 6th June 1944. My father, Jack Davis, was one such serving in the Second Northamptonshire Yeomanry which was deployed as the Armoured Reconnaissance Regiment of the Eleventh Armoured Division from 1943 until the Regiment was disbanded in mid-August 1944 with the surviving personnel being posted to other Armoured Formations.

It took a particular sort of bravery to fly these sorties, and consummate skill to handle the aircraft whilst directing the fire of the guns with which they were working. The teamwork required between the Pilot, his Observer/Wireless Operator, and the individual Gunners or Battery Commanders to achieve a successful shoot was remarkable. Yet sadly little is recorded in the many published histories, or in novels, about their work in the Second World War.

I am fortunate to own an Auster Mk V Alpha, a light aircraft which was built in 1944, but never issued to the Royal Air Force, eventually it was sold by the manufacturers in 1959 in a civilian configuration. I have enjoyed many hours flying her and other marks of the basic C G Taylor design built by the Auster Aeroplane Company and Beagle Ltd., formerly Taylorcraft, at Rearsby in Leicestershire, England. C G Taylor designs were also manufactured in the USA by the Taylorcraft Corporation and Piper Aircraft Corporation.

My greatest pleasure was to participate in the 50th Anniversary of D-Day celebrations Piloting my own Mark V Alpha; she and other Liaison aircraft participating were accommodated at, and flown from, a field that had been used in the battle for Normandy known as Advanced Landing Ground B7. This was located approximately midway between the villages of Vaux - sur - Seulles and Martragny, a few kilometres to the east of Bayeaux. All the participating aircraft and crews were given tremendous support by the Staff and General Aviation Pilots based at Caen Airport. To view the Landing Grounds, Battlefields, and Commonwealth War Graves Commission Cemeteries from the air whilst flying an aircraft of the type operated by the AOP Squadrons is a privilege enjoyed very few.

Anthony J Davis
Sandiacre, Nottingham
October 2024

Table of Contents

Part 1:

West Sussex, August 1967.

Chapter 1

Discovery

It was a gentle August morning, the sun rising over the South-downs was starting to disperse the tendrils of mist which hung in the lower areas of the landscape as Valentine Shooter, Val to his friends, walked to the gate of his mother's cottage garden and out onto the lane. It was quite a surprise for him to be out and about at such an early hour. As a University Student he was not accustomed to early morning exercise. Nevertheless, he had responded to the nagging voice in his head that had woken him from a hazily recalled dream. He didn't know where his feet would take him as he turned right and started up the slight rise towards the main road.

His mind was foggy with sleep still fighting for a hold over wakefulness. He walked without conscious thought as he sought to focus his mind on whatever had pulled him from his bed. Was it his future, or his past that had invaded his sleeping thoughts? He had been giving much thought to his immediate future over the past weeks following his graduation with a First-Class Honours Degree in Aeronautical Engineering from Cranfield University. His tutor had encouraged him to read for a Master's Degree, or better still a Research Doctorate. His studies had included learning to fly as a Private Pilot; he had gained his Private Pilot's Licence flying an Auster J5/F Aiglet, three of which were operated by the University. These were fully aerobatic training aircraft; high wing monoplanes which were equipped with a tailwheel rather than the more modern tricycle nose wheel configuration. They were powered by a single air-cooled de Havilland Gypsy Major inverted four-cylinder in-line engine which delivered one hundred and forty-five horsepower when at full throttle and in good condition. These aircraft being owned by the University were maintained in 'tip-top' condition.

The call of the skies was powerful. Val had also considered a career in the Royal Air Force as a Direct Entry Officer. He was the Son of a Pilot; his father Alexander James Shooter had served in the Royal Artillery during the Second World War, and at an early stage of hostilities had pressed his Commanding Officer to be allowed to train as an Air Observation Pilot at the earliest opportunity. Yesterday had been the anniversary of his father's death. He and his mother had spent time at his father's grave, which was maintained by the Commonwealth War Graves Commission, in the Church of England Cemetery at St Andrew's Church in Middle Down, West Sussex. Was that event also swirling about in his subconscious and unsettling him as he wandered along the road?

He had been walking for some time and the balmy morning coupled with the sounds of the countryside were working their calming effects. Valentine gradually started to become aware of his surroundings although he had no idea of exactly where he was. The sun was now much higher in the sky which was a glorious blue and streaked with mare's tail cirrus clouds. "How far have I come; how long have I been wandering?" he said to himself. He felt slightly uneasy as these thoughts crossed his mind, even more so as he had a sense of having been along that road at some time in the past but could not get his bearings or fix a time when he had been there. He pondered his situation; he had been born and raised locally by his widowed mother but had spent much of his formative years with his grandparents in Northamptonshire when he wasn't at his Junior Preparatory School at Nevill Holt in Leicestershire, before going to Oakham School in Rutland as a Boarder. This part of the area in which his mother had settled was not one that he had roamed as a child, nor yet in his youthful days of exploration whilst home from his School. Surprisingly, it seemed awfully familiar, but he couldn't place the area at all.

There was a copse of trees, mostly of Birch and Alder, a few hundred yards along the road that he felt wasn't quite how he thought it should be. He spotted a concrete track to the left and a gate on his right, to which he moved, giving him access to the woodland. It all seemed vaguely familiar to him as he moved towards it. However, the pair of modern five-barred gates across the track were not: shouldn't there be a wooden hut here? He looked back across the road; there should be group of huts there. He crossed the road and climbed the gate into the wooded space intent upon searching for clues as to where he was. It wasn't long before he came across spalling brick work that had once been the lower walls of a military hutment. Could this be the site of the former World War Two temporary aerodrome which was built in nineteen forty-two and used by the American Army Airforce in the latter years of the War? Of course! The realisation hit him with the sudden clarity. This was where his father had served as a Liaison Officer teaching American Airmen the Standard Operational Procedures used by British Army, its radio codes, and the navigation skills necessary for survival in the European Theatre of Operations.

He had stumbled upon the former RAF Upham Manor. Further exploration exposed some dilapidated buildings, broken concrete pathways and roads that interlinked them.

He decided to return to the road and look for the airfield site that couldn't be too far away. The concrete track leading to the new pair of five-barred gates had the look of a military road dating back to the nineteen forties. On reaching the gates, which were chained and padlocked, he stopped and gazed over the expanse of meadow before him. The concrete track broadened out forming a tee junction with a cracked and weed grown roadway that curved away both to the left and the right following the boundaries of the field. The sun was now much higher, the light was coming over his right shoulder casting a shadow to his left, he realised that he was looking northward straight along the principal axis of the meadow which was roughly rectangular. As he scanned the vista before him, he noticed a rectangular flat-topped structure at roughly the mid-point of the eastern perimeter before which lay a large area of concrete into which the roadway branching to his right gave access. At the nearer end of this apron, and set back towards the tree filled hedge, stood a large corrugated roofed shed that looked, from a distance, to be in reasonable repair. A second similar structure was even further back. This one seemed to be somewhat dilapidated and forlorn.

Curiosity, or was it that nagging voice again, had him climbing the right-hand gate close to the gatepost: as he did so he was able to see further into the field and he could make out a difference in the grass where it grew less lush in a straight line down the middle of the meadow on an approximately south to north alignment. He had found the aerodrome and saw the faint outline of the old runway. He could also discern the broken outlines of the frying pan dispersal points located around the perimeter that were connected by short stubby concrete tracks to the road, that he now recognised as the aerodrome perimeter track around which long since departed aircraft had taxied to and from the runway, the Firing-in Butts, and the Maintenance Hangars.

That voice in his subconscious intruded into his wondering mind. It was barely a whisper at first so that he hardly noticed it. However, it grew more insistent *"it's here, it's here – go and find it, you have to find it. It's here!"* Valentine dropped down inside the gate, he was starting to worry about what was happening to him. No matter that he was knowingly trespassing he was compelled to start along the wartime perimeter track towards what he now realised were the remains of the Watch Office, or Control Tower as it would be called at modern aerodromes. Why did it come to his mind as Watch Office? He started jogging eager to get there and find whatever the voice had urged him to discover. He realised that the corrugated roofed sheds would probably have been the aerodrome's maintenance hangars in the War: what on earth was drawing him to them?

As he drew closer to the old Watch Office, he saw that the ground floor windows and doors had been securely boarded up. He circled round to rear of the building discovering a very rusty steel stairway leading to a flat roof. Access to these stairs had been blocked off, obviously as a safety measure since they looked as though they would collapse under the weight of even a slightly built person: they certainly would not have supported Valentine's five-foot ten inch solidly built twelve stones. He moved on to investigate an adjacent single-story building that was not visible from the gates. The double doors on the front of this building were in good repair and had been recently painted with an olive-green military drab paint. These doors were secured with a hasp and padlock. He pushed his way through the tangled undergrowth that grew against the blank sidewalls and past the brambles in the hedge at the rear only to discover that a standard rear door, with a mortice lock, was also barred to him. The dirty metal framed, and barred, window next to the door mocked his attempts to see inside.

He felt desperately driven and ran to the corrugated arch of the large shed at the southern end of the apron of concrete. A pair of sliding doors were mounted across the front of this building. The doors were suspended from brackets to which sets of wheels were bolted: these engaged with overhead rails attached to the structural steel framing at the end of the building. The bottoms of the doors were fitted with rollers which ran in tracks embedded in the concrete of the apron. Short lengths of chain were welded to each of the doors, these were linked by the hasp of a large security padlock. A trip round this large shed showed that unauthorised access was not to be gained. There were translucent panels set on the roof some twenty feet or so above the ground. Valentine was relieved when he realised that there would be enough light inside for him to be able to see something of what was inside if he peered through the small gap in the metal sliding doors.

He strained to see what the shed might hold; his total being focussed on the strange exhortation he had heard in his mind *"find it – it's here."* He jumped, like one of the hares he had startled as he had jogged past it on his way to the apron area, as a gruff and angry voice shouted from a few feet behind him "what's your game then Sonny Jim, you're trespassing." Valentine spun round to face the owner of the voice, to be confronted with a stoutly built elderly man whose rather turnip shaped head was topped with a flat tweed cap beneath which wisps of iron-grey hair escaped. On his ruddy weather-beaten face an angry scowl was drawn. More worrying was the raised heavy Hawthorn stick held menacingly in the man's evidently strong right hand. Valentine looked the man squarely in the eye and said "I'm sorry if I have caused you any worry. I am not here to cause any trouble or damage. I somehow felt compelled to come here this morning to discover something. This will sound strange, but I honestly don't know for what I am looking, and even less why." The stout old man relaxed, lowered his powerful right arm, planted the stick firmly between his feet and leaning on it in towards Valentine he said "So why the hell should I believe that story? Who are you, and where are you from?" The old man looked at Valentine with a slightly puzzled look and momentarily the trace of a frown appeared, but he did not immediately relax his aggressive stance nor did the suspicious look completely disappear.

"My name is Valentine Shooter; I'm an Aeronautical Engineer and I am staying with my mother in Middle Down. I came out for walk this morning to clear my head and think about what I should do in the immediate future. I wandered completely aimlessly and found myself on the road outside the gate to the wood and the gates to this disused airfield, which I think must have been RAF Upham Manor. I felt drawn here, something in my subconscious half recognised the place but it seemed different. I had to explore. I started in the wood and then, standing at the gates to the field, I realised that what I was to discover was nearby. I realized that I might be trespassing. Nevertheless, I climbed the gate and came to investigate the buildings. It was obvious that they are used and my next move would have been to discover who owns the land and to obtain permission to investigate the buildings. As I said I meant no harm or to take anything away with me."

The older man looked steadfastly at Valentine's worried face for some seconds, it seemed like a lifetime to Valentine, before he stopped scowling. "I own the land" he said with a touch of pride in his voice. Slowly, as Valentine told his story of how his father's shot up aircraft had brought him home in August nineteen forty-four, the old man started to relax and became welcoming. He told Valentine that he was christened by George Albert Chamberlain, but he was known to all and sundry as Jasper. He explained that the land for aerodrome had been subject to compulsory acquisition by the Air Ministry in nineteen forty-two for use by the United States of America's Army Air Force. The RAF, and the USAAF, who moved in during the latter part of nineteen forty-three when the base facilities were completely ready for use, allowed the family to take crops of hay off the field in the non-operational   areas. The land was eventually returned to his family in nineteen forty-eight after the site had been cleared of military surplus and left on a 'Care and Maintenance' basis by the RAF, not that there had been any maintenance and precious little care. Then quite softly Jasper said, "I recall the name of Shooter." He paused deep in a reverie then continued "Captain Shooter, good name for an Artilleryman. He landed a little shot up 'plane here in forty-four. He died shortly after they got him and his already dead observer out of the kite." After a further and much longer pause he continued saying "I didn't witness his landing, or even see him, but the Yanks could talk of little else for quite a while. Some of them knew him well. He had been a Liaison Officer teaching them our ways and how to work on the battlefield with our troops." Now with a wistful look on his face he spoke, as if to himself. "So, you're his son. I should have recognised you, but it's been a long time." Valentine stood transfixed, unable to answer, he merely nodded his head whilst feeling close to tears.

Jasper then led Valentine to the old, somewhat battered, Willys Jeep in which he had sneaked up on his trespasser; with the engine off the only noise had been that of the tyres bumping over the cracks in the concrete and the soft squeak as the brakes were applied. "Now lad you look like you need a good stiff drink, and I certainly am in need of one." He paused then said "I'll take you to my local. We can get to know each other over a pint and a bite of lunch. How does that sound?"

Climbing into the driver's seat Jasper fired up the 2.4 litre Willys engine, engaged first gear, and let out the clutch just as Valentine was lowering himself into the canvass covered, steel framed, passenger seat. "Sorry, she's none too comfortable a ride lad. But she's special to me and I won't use anything else about the farm." chuckled Jasper, noting Valentine's discomfiture.

Chapter 2

Friendship

Jasper drove the couple of miles up the road away to the north of the old airfield towards his home village of Upham. During the journey he opened up a little to Valentine giving him a short resume of his life. Upham Manor Farm had been in the hands of the Chamberlain family for generations; Jasper's father had been greatly concerned when his son had joined the Royal Engineers in nineteen fourteen and the subsequent posting to serve as a Private with No 1 Balloon Company in Flanders. He had managed to get a transfer to the Royal Flying Corps in nineteen sixteen as an airframe rigger and was transferred into the newly formed Royal Air Force on the first of April nineteen eighteen. He returned to the farm after the Great War and, with his father, he had built it up through the years of the Great Depression until the start of the Second World War by which time it was a thriving modern agricultural business. Everything changed as Britain was encouraged to become self-sufficient in feeding the nation; later the farm's best meadowland had been requisitioned for military use. When the airfield construction teams moved onto the farm it had been a race to get the hay crop off the meadows that became RAF Upham Manor. He had pleaded and argued his case that the land not taken over for runways, taxiways and roadways should be left to grow and that he should take a hay crop off it for the war effort. Officialdom eventually relented and a good working relationship grew up between the Chamberlains, the RAF Liaison people, and the USAAF personnel operating at the Airbase. Jasper broke off his story and announced, "here we are" as he swung the Jeep off the road into the drive and yard of the Old White Hart Inn which was located on Main Street in the centre of the village opposite the Green. The village inn, built entirely of stone with slate roofing, had served the good yeomen of the Parish of Upton for centuries, as well as being a haven for travellers making their way across the Downs. It was a substantial building, or rather an amalgam of conjoined buildings, including stables, storerooms, a dairy, and a piggery. All of which were set alongside a stoned yard and lawned garden which lay on the southern aspect of the property. Extensions had been added bit by bit, over centuries of development, to the original medieval ale house turning it into the current characterful Inn. As Valentine jumped out of the Jeep, and moved across the yard's entrance, he noticed the different architectural styles and uneven roof lines. Jasper parked the Jeep outside the front door in a rectangular area formed by the two parts of the building that fronted Main Street and overlooked the Green. Long in the past the Green had been a thriving marketplace now it was a recreation area with the remains of the Market Cross standing at its centre.

The gable end wall facing the village green lay roughly parallel with the road; there had originally been a small window in that wall to one side of the great chimney which rose within the stonework. The window had been infilled with stone, the outline of which still stood out from the surrounding masonry, no doubt lost as victim to a long defunct "Window Tax." Two large Georgian style sash windows were let into the south frontage on both the ground and upper floors respectively, between which an untidy climbing rose bush grew to the eves. Directly in front of the now parked Jeep an east facing wall was pierced, at ground floor level by two small gate-style windows both of which were partially open to allow the air to circulate inside. Above them was a much larger more recently installed modern three panelled gate window.

Jasper led the way through the open door into a tiny hallway: directly in front of them rose a flight of stairs leading to guest rooms and the landlord's private quarters on the first floor. To the right a door opened onto a long spacious dining room dominated by a great table set with twenty places. Against the long back wall, centrally located, stood a large mahogany sideboard covered with a snow-white cloth upon which sat serving dishes, coffee and teapots, hot water flasks, milk and cream jugs, and sugar bowls. The wall at the far end of the room held a generous fireplace set with kindling ready to be lit. The fire-grate stood in the centre of a great chimney breast, on either side of which cosy inglenooks were filled with a pair of club style armchairs and occasional tables.

Jasper turned to left through an open doorway and as he did so he called over his shoulder "mind the step." They entered a room, smaller than the dining room opposite, which had the title of Smoke Room over the door. It was furnished with leather button-backed club armchairs grouped around low rustic dark oak tables giving an air of a gentleman's club lounge. A small servery was set on the long wall to their right behind which was the Inn's well stocked bar, curiously called The Cellar even though it was entirely at ground level. The Smoke Room, although deceptively snug, was quite generously proportioned. This and the adjacent Cellar were the oldest part of the Inn, the walls were not less than two feet thick with the southern wall being rather deeper, having a floor to ceiling cupboard set into it to the right of the hearth. There was no need of a fire in the grate since the day was pleasantly warm outside. However, within these thick walls the room was cool but comfortably so. The room jutted out into the drive forming an "L" shape with the dining room and entrance hall; the windows, beneath which the Jeep sat at rest, gave a good view of the Green. On the far side of which stood a large Georgian house and a small, detached cottage to the right of that building. Behind these houses the ground rose slightly to the crest of the downland on the southern slopes of which the village sprawled its length.

Jasper motioned Valentine to a chair in the window alcove to the left of the fireplace whilst he rapped on the servery shelf to bring the bar staff to take his order. A pretty young woman, devoid of makeup, with her long chestnut coloured hair tied back in a ponytail greeted him warmly and asked who the handsome young man sitting at the window might be. "That we shall have to find more of. Suffice to say I'm minded to believe that he must be a relative of an old friend of your grandad from the wartime. We'll find out well enough over our lunch. Now, what's the best you can do for us today my girl?" "Well sir, we have some well-seasoned gammon from that porker of yours that Walter Jefferson slaughtered for us. That comes with mashed spuds and kidney beans fresh from the garden this morning and homemade parsley sauce. You'll want a pint of Grandad's Home Brewed to go with it of course, and we have a lovely apple pie and custard for a pud' if you can handle it." Jasper turned to Valentine and said, "how does that sound to you young feller?" Valentine replied, "I missed my breakfast, I'll eat whatever the lass puts in front of me: and home brewed sounds wonderful." "Two pints of Grandad's best it is then" said the barmaid turning to a cask that was sitting, with several others, on a thrawl behind her. Holding a pewter pint pot beneath the brass tap and turning it on produced a desultory gurgling noise, a dribble of a dark amber liquid spluttered into Jasper's tankard. She reached for a mallet that hung over the casks and gave the spial peg in the bung on the top of the barrel a sharp rap to one side, the peg loosened, and the dark beer flowed smoothly into Jasper's personal pot. She called to Valentine "do you want a straight glass or one with a handle?" "Handle please" was his instant reply. The beer mugs filled to the brim, with a small necklace of bubbles clinging on the meniscus round the rims, were placed carefully on the bar. Jasper took a deep draught from his tankard before carefully making his way to the table where Valentine was ensconced.

After a period of silence in which both men drew on their beer, each with his own thoughts, Valentine suddenly exclaimed "I know this place! How can that be? I don't think that I've ever been to Upham in my life?" The barmaid who had been quietly watching Valentine looked surprised and called over to him "that's strange, do you often have a sense of déjà vu?" "Not until now" he said after a short pause during which a worried look fell across his face. "In fact, it has happened twice today already." Valentine fell silent as he contemplated the events of that most unusual morning.

His thoughts were soon pushed aside as a slightly stooped elderly gentleman approached their table with a large tray in his hands. On his tray were two oval platters under shining silvery covers beside which sat a cruet set and two sets of cutlery wrapped in creamy white linen napkins. The old man had a narrow, sharp featured, face topped with a patch of thinning grey hair. His body was as lean as a rail, with skin like the bark on a Hazel bough. "What's this? Personal VIP service Charlie? What's brought that about?" chafed Jasper as his old friend, the Landlord of the Inn, laid their meals before them. "Young Jeannie told Mother and me that you had a guest that might be related to an old friend from wartime days; I weren't sure which war you were speaking of so I decided that I would bring the food me'self and find out." Charlie looked hard at Valentine with a vague light of recognition starting to form in his eyes. He went on to say, "as for the VIP treatment Mother insisted that if your guest was special, we must treat him right." After a lengthy pause in which Charlie looked intently at Valentine he quietly, almost reverently, said "I am beginning to think that he could well be a very special young man." Then more loudly and cheerfully he stated, "now enough chit-chat and get yourselves outside the best home cooked meal you'll get for miles around."

They had all but finished their meal, which had been eaten in companiable silence, for it was too good let go cold whilst they conversed, when the door in the far side of the room swung open and well-built man who had the looks of one well used to being outdoors and was no stranger to hard and heavy work made an appearance. He looked to be in his mid to late his forties. He entered carrying a platter loaded with a ploughman's lunch complimented with several hunks of thick, crusty, home baked brown bread, homemade chutney together with a packet of potato crisps in one hand and a half empty pint 'jug' of ale in the other. He greeted Jasper with a smile and a twinkle in his eyes. "Hello dad! Fancy finding you in here, public bar not good enough anymore? Ashamed that the lads might be a bit rough and coarse for your new friend here?" Jasper laughed, "no lad I just wanted to have some peace and quiet whilst we got to know each other over a pint and a good lunch. Join us, draw up a chair; but before you do ask Charlie over if has the time." Valentine stood and put out a hand to Jasper's son, who having already put his lunch on the table, took it firmly in his powerful grip and shook it vigorously whilst introducing himself as Giles. "Let me introduce myself, I'm Valentine Shooter, I've been staying with my mother in Middle Down for the Summer since I finished my aeronautical engineering degree course at Cranfield University. Your father found me exploring the old Upham Manor aerodrome buildings; he thought I was up to no good until I sort of explained. He brought me here so that he could hear more of how I came to be trespassing on his land." "Ah, right! You sort of explained? What do you mean by that?" Queried Jasper's son with a puzzled frown above his penetrating bright blue eyes: a look which gave the impression of an astute man used to command. "To be perfectly frank, I don't really know how I got to the aerodrome or what drove me to explore first the woods and then the buildings where your father found me." He paused for a few seconds and continued "I had woken early and felt compelled to go out for a walk to clear my brain and decide upon my future career. I wandered without noticing where I was going, or what was going on around me, until I spotted the gate into the woods and the concrete roadway leading to the aerodrome gates." Another pause, longer this time, and then he continued in a rather puzzled and pensive tone. "I sensed something familiar about the place, but I just couldn't put my finger on it. I just had to explore the site as a voice in my head kept repeating find it – it's here. It's so strange, spooky even, I began to think I must be going 'doolally'!" Another period of silence, and then he said very slowly but quite forcibly "What the hell is happening here? Can any of you shed any light on it?"

Charlie had joined the group as Valentine had been speaking, he smiled gently and exchanged an almost imperceptible glance with the other two men. With a serious, but friendly, look on his lean face he stared at Valentine for a second or two then said somewhat profoundly, "Mr Shooter you are amongst old friends, and new." Valentine started from his chair surprised that the landlord knew his name "I didn't introduce myself and I don't think Jasper or Giles mentioned it! How do you know my name; and which old friends?"

"You are the spitting image of Captain Alex Shooter, who was a good friend of mine and our locals back in forty-three and four. I'm guessing, but am quite certain, that you are his son. Alex used to bring his American buddies here to unwind of an evening when they were all done at the airbase, that's what the Yanks called it." He paused and then continued with a wistful smile. "They called your dad Cap'n Hotshot, they really took to him and were quite broken up when he was posted back to his Squadron in time for the Invasion: D-Day." Valentine sat there absolutely shaken to the core, speechless, and looking totally bemused. Charlie thought for a moment before saying with a broad grin on his narrow face, "I've got somethings I'd like show you if you will wait just a minute whilst I go to our private quarters to fetch them."

Valentine remained motionless, intrigued by what he had just heard. He had never known his father; he had been born on the fourteenth of February nineteen forty-five, seven months after his father had died in action. Of course, he had learned about his father from his mother, Uncle Ollie, and his grandparents. He was immensely proud to be the son of such a fine soldier and well-respected person. There was obviously more to learn about his father and his exploits, doubtless some of which were unknown to his family. "What a day" he thought to himself. "Where is all this going to lead, I wonder?" Jasper and Giles moved away to the servery to have Jeannie refill their glasses, and to leave Valentine with his thoughts. It was also an opportunity to have a quiet word together regarding this morning's strange turn events and what might next transpire.

Chapter 3

Revelation

Charlie returned with an old square biscuit tin in his hands. "Now look'ee here, this is real treasure trove for you young Mr Shooter" he exclaimed as he placed the tin on the table in front of Valentine. "What?" chortled Valentine, reading the faded script on the lid. "A tin of Jacob's cream crackers that must be at least as old as I am!" Charlie laughed with him and said, "Open it you crackpot; crackers be damned." Valentine gripped the tin and levered the lid free. He had no idea of what he would find, but he had a good feeling about what would be revealed to him. The first thing he saw was a yellowing card that was about the size of modern A4 sheet of paper. A title 'Upham Manor 1944' was top and centre, beneath that a dozen or so signatures were scrawled on it. One written in a flourishing hand, in the centre of the lower part of the card, stated Captain Alex Shooter MC RA. The others were in a different style of writing, a standard cursive script not entirely dissimilar to copperplate but in a more modern form, with which Valentine was not familiar. Not all the names were easy to decipher, and some were definitely not of British origin. "A group photograph" he thought as he turned the card over in his hands. The black and white photograph mounted within the studio type card frame was as sharp and clear as the day it was first printed some twenty-three years earlier. The image showed a group of smiling young men in military uniforms looking into the camera. Some were standing, and others kneeling, in front a small single-enginede high-wing monoplane which was parked up on a concrete apron that was backed by woodland.

A handsome young man wearing British Army battledress, with his cap pushed to the back and slightly to one side of his head, was at the centre of the group. He was leaning nonchalantly on the left side engine cowling of the little 'plane, his left hand on his hip and his right on the propeller.

Valentine was transfixed; he was looking at his double! There were quite a few photographs of Alex Shooter in the family album at home but none which had the powerful emotional effect of this image. He took a second or two before softly saying "Dad! That's my dad" as tears welled in his eyes. He could not tear his gaze away from his dad's image to register the other young Officers in the photograph, all of whom were wearing their best US Army Air Force uniforms 'pinks' as they were called. One man in the picture was slightly older than the rest: he was dressed in pale-drab blouse and pants with the chevrons of a Master Sergeant on the sleeves of his blouse. He was standing to left of Alex Shooter and behind the lift-struts that were attached to the undercarriage at the lower end and at the upper end to the wing approximately two thirds of the way to the wing tip. This man was leaning forward with his hands on the struts as if about to push the aircraft forward in readiness for flight. Jasper leaned over Valentine's shoulder and pointed out the Master Sergeant, saying to the assembled company, "top man there; Joe Kennedy, he was a crew chief and one of the best men to wear the uniform, we were great pals. Weren't we Charlie?" Charlie nodded saying "yes." Jasper continued, "he was a really caring man, totally committed to his charges: his airplanes, Grasshoppers as he called them, and to his boys. He couldn't abide waste and would repair, rework, and then squirrel away spares and parts that others would have tossed into the scrap bin. He was such a respected lad that the Officers turned a blind eye to his coming in here with them; fraternisation between Officers and enlisted men was not encouraged in those days." Jasper continued "we stay in touch exchanging Christmas cards and the odd letter. I must admit I rather miss him; we owe him a lot."

Jasper went on to tell the story how of how he and Joe Kennedy first met and how their friendship developed. In early nineteen forty-two a man from the Air Ministry arrived at the farm with papers to serve regarding the compulsory purchase of land either side of the Middle Down Road; the Chamberlains were instructed to vacate the site. The site boundaries were marked on a map attached to the Purchase Order. Work to build an aerodrome, and a domestic site, for the use of the American Army Air Force was scheduled to commence before the Winter set in. The largest parcel of land, lying to the north of the road, was a reasonably flat meadow close to the crest of the Downs. This meadow was designated as a satellite landing ground under the control of the Station Commander at RAF Tangmere located on the south coast not too many miles distant. The Chamberlains played a 'war effort' card in their dealings with the man from the Ministry pointing out that the meadow was due to be cut for hay as winter-feed for their livestock and went further by suggesting that once established the greater part of the land would not be used for aircraft taking off, landing, or taxying so perhaps there could be an arrangement under which they could continue to take a hay crop off the field for the duration of hostilities. The cropping of the meadow before construction work started was agreed immediately, and after a bit of 'toing and froing' the RAF and USAAF agreed to further cropping, and storage, of the hay after training operations had become established at the newly commissioned RAF Upham Manor. An American Airfield Construction Unit quickly cleared the designated domestic and technical sites and had useable prefabricated buildings erected in a matter of weeks.

A maze of concrete roads and pathways threaded through, and around, the site which had been bounded by new fencing. A concrete apron had been laid and the floor plans for the maintenance hangars and the aerodrome Watch Office were also cast in concrete on the eastern side of the meadow. To the south of these another expanse of concrete was laid for motor transport garages. Underground storage tanks for petrol, diesel and aviation spirit were installed along with the pumps required to fill the bowsers from which the aircraft, and vehicles, would be refuelled. To the north of the hangars a compass swinging base was built to provide a place in which there was no magnetic interference from the structures where the aircraft compasses could be calibrated. Over on the western side of the field a further stand-alone complex of structures was built that would become the ammunition dump, the 'firing in' butts for the harmonisation of aircraft machine guns, and twenty-five yard 'barrack range' for small arms practice. Much to the Chamberlain's relief the construction unit did not plough up the meadow to build concrete runways, instead interlocking pierced steel planks were laid along the north-south axis of the meadow to form the main runway, with a secondary runway of the same construction being laid on a northeast-southwest alignment.

Whilst many of the locals resented the sudden appearance of the brash young Americans disrupting their quiet little world Jasper went out of his way to cultivate good relations with them, especially the USAAF Base Commander, and the RAF Liaison Officer. These two men, Lieutenant-Colonel Gene Monson and Squadron Leader Archie Cross, were to be essential allies if the farm was to be able to use at least part of the land that had been taken from their control. Colonel Monson was the son of rancher and had a good understanding of Jasper's position. Eventually he managed to have his Supply Officer negotiate an agreement with the Ministry of Food and the US Army to buy local produce from Jasper, and other local farmers, as a supplement to their standard ration allowances.

Not long afterwards the aerodrome opened and aircraft of several diverse types, together with their ground crews, started to arrive to build up the training fleet. Then there was an influx of young American aircrew eager to become operational in the skies over the European Continent. The majority of these young Pilots were destined to fly small unarmed Liaison aircraft, but there were some whose training was to for a very different role. These slightly older and more experienced airmen flew the North American A7 Apache Ground Attack fighters. The arrival caused quite stir at the base, and amongst the local lads who spent their spare time watching the comings and goings of the aircraft whilst chatting with the ground crew working on the dispersal pans close to the boundary fences. A handful of experienced Royal Air Force and Army Gunner Pilots were seconded in to act as Instructors and teach the eager beaver Americans the operational and radio procedures that would allow them to integrate into the planned combined operations that would carry them across the English Channel to fight alongside their allies.

In the main the 'Yanks' were cocksure, devil may care, types who thought they knew it all until they had flown a few training sorties. They found low level navigation over the English countryside disorientating, and they frequently became lost in an extraordinarily short time after take-off. They quickly found out that there was a language problem. The Americans' ears were not attuned to the dialects and accents of the British Control Officers, nor did they have a good understanding of the phonetic alphabet and code words used by the British and Allied forces. These, they learned very quickly thanks to their British Instructors. Captain Shooter was one of the best and the most respected of the bunch. The air, and ground, crews in his flight took to him since he had a straightforward way with people and took time to ensure that their training and general wellbeing was of the highest order.

Jasper went on to explain that he had little contact with the operational people on the base apart from Joe Kennedy who was the senior Master Sergeant assigned to look after him and his farmhands, two of whom were Land Girls serving in the Women's Land Army. Joe took a fatherly role with the girls. He made it his job to protect them from the lewd and rapacious advances of his young countrymen as best he could. Joe was a mid-westerner who had grown up in the dustbowl states and had learned to fix anything from a leaky faucet to a water pump engine or a reaping machine; in short anything on the family farm. He could work with almost any materials to make-do and mend; mostly using hand-tools and simple hand-cranked machines or, for those that were belt-driven, from a power take-off drive fitted to a tractor. Joe was always reluctant to scrap anything that could be remotely considered as repairable or could be stripped for spare parts. By the end of the war, he had built up quite a collection of useful bits and pieces that didn't appear on any inventory. This collection included the Jeep that was now owned by Jasper. At the end of the American tenure of RAF Upham Manor in nineteen forty-six Joe had been ordered by Colonel Monson to dispose of everything that couldn't be returned to the central stores. Joe did this by giving it away to the local farmers and garage owners, to keep things legal he provided impressive looking 'Certificates of Disposal' showing the legal transfer of ownership from the USAAF to the recipient. Once the USAAF left the site it reverted to the RAF, and it was placed on a 'Care and Maintenance' basis. Squadron Leader Cross was posted to RAF Tangmere effective from the last day of American occupation and all that remained was a small team of Administration and Technical Staff to oversee the rundown of the station. RAF Upham Manor, together with the remaining buildings and everything within them, ceased to exist as far as officialdom was concerned and the site was transferred back to the ownership of the Chamberlain Family in the Spring of nineteen forty-eight.

Part 2

Rutland, Somerset and Wiltshire 1937 ~ France 1939/40 ~ Hampshire June 1941 ~ West Sussex 1943/44, and Normandy June ~ August 1944.

Chapter 4

Aux Armes, Mes Amis

The late Mid-summer of nineteen thirty-seven was idyllic for members of Oakham School's Upper Sixth Form for their end of year examinations were over. For most of the boys their final year at school had been designed to prepare them for the rites of passage to university entry, or a career in one or other of the Military Services. Their days, as they awaited the end of the Summer term, were filled with a comfortable lifestyle enjoying sports, athletics, swimming in the unheated open-air pool, cricket and the domestic realities of living in their respective schoolhouses. The Officer Cadet Training Corps members were preparing their personal and corps kit in readiness for the up-coming Summer Camp. Alexander James Shooter, Alex, and his closest pal William Oliver Squires, Ollie, came from military families and farming stock. Both were keenly looking forward to their last camp with the School's OCTC which was to be held in Somerset on the Mendip Hills at the Yoxter Training Camp.

The rationale for the OCT, which was established in eighteen fifty-nine as a Volunteer Corps in the independent 'public' schools in Great Britain was one of preparing young men to face the world by providing training in a disciplined organisation within schools promoting the qualities of responsibility, self-reliance, resourcefulness, endurance and perseverance so that pupils might develop powers of leadership that would be of benefit to them and their country. One of the principal objectives of the OCT was to 'encourage those who have an interest in the Services to become Officers of the Regular or Reserve Forces.' Whilst the OCT was strictly a Volunteer Corps the ethos at Oakham School was very much one of 'join willingly when of suitable age and physical capability or reconsider being a pupil at this school.' Alex and Ollie had been very enthusiastic joiners and active participants. They revelled in the basic infantry training that was the mainstay of their activities and were excited when opportunities to see, and sometimes participate in, the work of other arms of the Military Services when presented: especially whilst attending the annual week-long Summer camps. During their time with the OCTC they had taken the opportunity to learn to fly gliders at the local Gliding Club and were competent solo Pilots. Both had developed an interest in gunnery and felt drawn to the Artillery; hardly surprising since artillerymen featured in each of their extended families. Both young men had a scientific bent and regularly scored highly in the end of term mathematics and science examinations.

Summer camp at Yoxter had been great fun, but there was a shadow laid over the event as the political situation on the European Continent became increasingly strained. Adolf Hitler, the German Chancellor, and his senior National Socialist Party associates were making increasingly inflammatory speeches about the enemies of the Reich, the Jews and other non-Aryan peoples, and the need for room into which the German nation could expand. Several of the school leavers that Summer had recognised that the armed forces would soon be in need of trained Officers and had opted to join the Services rather than continue their education at University. Alex and Ollie, with the unconditional support of their parents, had put in their papers to join the Royal Corps of Artillery and received their orders to report to the Royal School of Artillery at Larkhill in Wiltshire only a week after they had left their OCT camp at Yoxter.

Having completed the standard basic training during their school days in the OCT they were exempt from the initial training that raw recruits were required to undergo before going on to their technical and basic Officer training courses. Both Alex and Ollie had decided at an early stage that they wanted to have the glamour, excitement and relative freedom of action that was to be found in the Field Artillery. The Field Regiments and the Royal Horse Artillery had the task of providing mobile close support to the infantry. They applied for places, which were granted, on the requisite courses. Once the courses were successfully behind them, they were commissioned as Second Lieutenants in the Royal Field Artillery and posted to their respective Regiments.

On the third of September nineteen thirty-nine the Prime Minister, Mr Neville Chamberlain, announced to the world that the German Government had failed to comply with a requirement to withdraw their troops from the Poland and that a state of war existed between Great Britain and Germany. The Regular Army, the Royal Air Force, and the Royal Navy were fully mobilised: the Reserve Forces were called to operational status and additional manpower was rapidly conscripted. Ollie was serving with the 2004th Field Regiment which was ready for service with the British Expeditionary Force and was to be sent to France with immediate effect. Alex called his chum on the telephone for a chat and to pick up whatever 'gen' there was to be had about what was known about the 'Hun' action on the Continent. The short answer, from Ollie, to his questions was simple. "You know about as much as I do old boy. I just know that we are trying to pull together maps of northern France, and the Regimental Intelligence Officer is tearing about in a real tizzy trying to find out if the 'Hun' is making any moves against the Maginot Line."

Alex's Regiment spent several months through the winter and early Spring of nineteen thirty-nine and nineteen forty bringing the Regiment up to full strength and learning how to handle the new quick firing Twenty-five Pounder field guns that were being issued to replace their old Great War Eighteen Pounders: some of which had been upgraded to fire Twenty-five Pounder ammunition as an interim measure. The newly recruited gunners, who had received their basic and initial technical training, had to be worked up to become efficient members of the gun-crews capable of undertaking the roles of all other members of their crew. With the new guns came the Quad tractors and limbers to haul the guns across country to their action stations. Crews learned to drive and maintain the assembly of Quad tractor-limber-gun in all manner of conditions and how to get the guns ready to fire as quickly and effectively as possible. Also, how to get them on the move as fast as practicable to take up new firing positions when necessary. This training was later to prove its worth when Alex's Battery was in severe danger of being destroyed by enemy action in France. As a Battery Officer Alex had a twenty-eight hundredweight Morris truck together with a dedicated Driver assigned to him. This vehicle carried two radio sets and two Signallers were detailed to operate them.

The 'Phoney War' had dragged on into the Spring of nineteen forty; Ollie and Alex exchanged occasional letters in this period of 'calm before the storm.' Ollie was getting restless and told Alex that keeping his Troop 'on their toes' when there were so many places for recreation involving 'wine, women, and song' quite close to the Battery Lines was a 'job-and-a-half'. The casualties' wounds were generally self-inflicted as a direct result of over-indulgence in the recreational activities both on the playing fields as well as in the local public bars, and other less savoury establishments. This came to an abrupt stop once the German Army made its first moves in the west, attacking through Belgium and the Low Countries. Alex's Regiment was placed on immediate standby, with orders to prepare for embarkation. Within a week an Advance Party, including Alex, had landed in France and were ordered to survey ground along the section of the Franco-Belgian border into which the Infantry Division with which they were tasked to work would be deployed.

There was little or no time to settle into any semblance of a peacetime encampment. The Brigade and Regimental Headquarters, together with the Regimental Wagon Lines, were set up a few miles south of the French town of Maubeuge on the River Sambre. The Batteries were deployed, dug in, along a twelve-mile-long section of the N440 highway between Sartiau in the southeast and Quevy in the northwest. The Twenty-five Pounder guns could provide fire to cover ground for up to seven and a half miles to their front, and thus they provided overlapping fire support along a line which stretched from Mons to Castillion. Other guns of both Medium and Heavy Regiments were deployed as part of the Divisional Artillery in the same sector. When the German forces thrust through the Ardennes Forest, bypassing the mighty Maginot Line's fortifications, the French forces facing them were forced to retreat and orders were issued to Alex's battery to relocate to a newly prepared position closer to Charleroi near Binche on the N90. Once established the Battery Major asked for a volunteer to go forward to establish contact with the Infantry deployed across their front. Alex immediately stepped out and accepted the task. His truck had mysteriously disappeared, it had last been seen heading off towards the town.

There was no other transport immediately available so he set out on foot. In the village of Waudrez he came across the local Postman from whom he commandeered a bicycle. He continued through the town of Binche and eventually found an Infantry Company who were digging-in to create a defensive position on either side of the road at a crossroads on the outskirts of Anderlues. The Infantry Company Sergeant Major told him that they had intelligence that the Germans were crossing the River Sambre in Charleroi and that there were rumours of enemy armoured reconnaissance units advancing along the N90 towards their position. Alex thanked the CSM and told him that his Battery were five miles to the west and well positioned to provide counter-attacking fire. The CSM assured Alex that they were in radio contact with the Divisional HQ and that if needed they would call for supporting fire from the Division. With that Alex jumped on his bicycle and furiously pedalled back to his Battery, whilst only a few miles away from the infantry position he heard shelling from the east and surmised the enemy must already have broken through Charleroi and were advancing along the N90. This information was passed to his Battery Commander and he returned to his own troops ordering them to immediate readiness to provide supporting fire to the infantry at Anderlues. The field telephone system linking the Regiment's Batteries to the Brigade has not yet been established and radio communications were intermittent. Alex reported to the Battery Major offering to go forward to act as a Forward Observer to direct fire as necessary. Neither his truck, nor its crew, was still anywhere to be found. He grabbed a spare 38 set, a personal radio that was contained in a backpack, with which to communicate with the Battery Commander until his signallers could establish a field telephone connection to his Forward Observation Post. He again set of on his commandeered bicycle and was quickly calling down fire onto advancing enemy armour before calling for the guns to withdraw as fast as possible to prevent them from being overrun.

Alex had no idea where his Battery had been sent, his radio calls went unanswered. He scouted back towards Maubeuge, fighting with the Infantry in rearguard skirmishes along the way. Eventually he managed to rejoin one of his Troops. The whole of the BEF was being forced to make a fighting withdrawal towards Dunkirk. Despite the chaos of the retreat to the Dunkirk Perimeter Alex managed to keep his new Troop together and amazingly they eventually linked up with their Battery whilst fighting desperate rearguard actions. In the congested and shrinking defensive Perimeter they again lost contact with their Battery, and the Regiment. Alex set up a defensive position on the northern edge of the Perimeter and maintained a bombardment of enemy positions which were identified by the Infantry Reconnaissance Platoon that had dug-in around his guns. When ammunition stocks were no longer being replenished Alex ordered his Gunners to destroy their guns and retreat to the beaches with the infantry who had bravely remained with them.

The crew of a small Fishing Smack picked them up off the beach, Alex insisted on being the last man of the Troop to be rescued. Back in England the Regiment was licking its wounds but was far from beaten. They re-equipped as fast as practicable with the new guns, limbers and tractors which were being provided from the factories in the Midlands and the North. New recruits fresh from the School of Artillery soon had the Regiment at its full complement and training was proceeding to the satisfaction of both the Colonel and the Brigadier. Promotion from acting Lieutenant to Lieutenant was a pleasant surprise to Alex, but this was nothing compared with personal congratulations from his Battery Major on 'a job well done' and then from his Colonel who told him that he had been 'Mentioned in Dispatches' for his actions in France. The Colonel also hinted that he really should be 'getting a gong,' and that he should look to the pages of the London Gazette. Alex was both pleased as punch and very humbled when he saw himself gazetted for the award of a Military Cross which was awarded, in front of his parents, by the King himself.

Chapter 5

New beginnings.

By late nineteen forty-one Alex was getting restless and was looking for opportunities to develop his skills. He had been studying the latest 'gen' regarding the Art of Gunnery and the role of the Forward Observation Posts on the Battlefield. He realised that this war was not going to be the static slogging match that had characterised the previous war with Germany and that a more fluid and responsive method of directing the guns would be needed. He gave considerable thought to new developments that were quite literally 'in the air' and he had several discussions with his fellow Officers; especially so with his Battery Major. So it was that one morning Alex marched up to his Commanding Officer's door, rapped upon it, and when summonsed by a curt "enter" he quickly complied and coming to attention he threw up a crisp salute. "Sir, you asked to see me" he said. Lieutenant Colonel Sir Julian Willoughby-Waterleys drew on his briar pipe for a second or two and then said, "yes Shooter, I did. Your Battery Major tells me that you wish to be considered for training as an Air Observation Post Pilot. Tell me, what has brought on this restlessness, or should I say recklessness? It's a damn dangerous occupation sitting up there for the Boche to shoot holes in you." "Sir," responded Alex, "I have been studying the work done by Major Bazeley and the RAF working with the French Army before the fall of France, and I am aware that forward spotting in the line has limitations when judging the fall of shot, or the identification of the location of guns engaged in counter-battery fire on our own positions." Alex paused for a second or two as he developed his argument. He continued, "Part of General McNaughton's work in the Great War demonstrated the value of aerial reconnaissance in gathering up-to-date intelligence to give Battery Commanders a better opportunity to site their guns and concentrate their fire on pre-selected targets. I am convinced that Air Observation will be an important part of beating the Nazi regime; and I believe that I have the right attributes to make a positive contribution. I have Piloting experience in gliders gained on a week-long advanced glider Piloting course in North Yorkshire whilst I was a Cadet in the Officer Cadet Training Corps at Oakham. My gunnery record is of a good standard, and I have an aptitude for the science and mathematics relating to the Art of Gunnery." Alex continued, "there has been a call for volunteers to form a nucleus of trained Gunner Pilots from within the Army Cooperation Squadrons. I am requesting permission to volunteer." "Humm: I can see, and hear, your eagerness in the way you have approached this. As you are probably aware the RAF and Corps of the Royal Artillery have plans already in hand to set up three Squadrons operating small, unarmed aeroplanes; our chaps are the Pilots, Observers, Signallers, and MT Types. The RAF will provide the Technical Staff, Supply, and Admin Staff." He continued, "you are a good chap to have around Shooter; but since you are so keen, I'll see what we can do to get you sent over for assessment as a Trainee Pilot. Good luck my boy, you are going to need it. Oh, and be aware that the newly forming Airborne Brigade are on the lookout for Army Types that can be trained as Glider Pilots, with your background they will want to snaffle you from us" With grin Alex retorted "hopefully I can make the case that as a dedicated Gunner I shall be more useful as an Air Observation Pilot than as a Glider Driver, sir." "Good man" said the Colonel "Dismiss." "Sir" responded Alex, saluting, and making a neat about turn he let himself out the office. The thought ran through his head "well I'm blowed, the old man is actually going to support my application for transfer to AOP training and posting, if I can cut the mustard." He was overjoyed that the chance to prove himself in the new branch of intelligence gathering and controlling shoots looked as though it would be his.

The following week he was dispatched to London, and the RAF Medical Centre on Regent Street, where he was subjected to a searching series of tests, examinations, and an interview before being pronounced as fit for 'General Duties' grade A1. Six weeks after his interview with Lt-Colonel Willoughby-Waterleys a simple entry in Daily Orders, announced, *effective Monday 10-11-41, Lt A J Shooter MC posted 22 EFTS Cambridge, training.* Alex jumped for joy and rushed off to the Officer's Mess to share the news with his fellow Subalterns, to celebrate his good fortune, and to have his Batman prepare his kit for the move scheduled just four days hence. That evening he wrote letters to his parents telling them of his impending career change and to his best friend, Ollie Squires, from his school days at Oakham telling him of the new opportunity that was his. He also suggested that it would be 'absolutely wizard' if they could both become AOP Pilots. He indirectly dropped a hint as to where he was being posted for training by stating that he would be just down the road from Ollie's older sister, Jane, in her cloistered Halls of Academia at Newnham College in Cambridge.

His last days with the Regiment were a whirl of activity. He still had his normal daily duties to discharge including Duty Officer, attending lectures on such subjects as 'gas attack and the precautions that must be taken to avoid being overcome by it,' 'Forward Observation Post actions prior to and during a shoot' and 'signals.' His last task was an unofficial trip to the motor transport pool to scrounge a tankful of petrol, plus spare full tin, for his little Austin Seven car to enable him to drive from the Battery at Lyndhurst in the New Forest, Hampshire, to Cambridge on Sunday morning. He had already contacted the Presidents of the respective Officers' Messes, and the Accommodation Officers, letting them know his travel plans and an approximate arrival time in Cambridge. On arrival at a manor house near Stow-cum-Quy situated two and a half miles to the northeast of Cambridge Airport he was greeted by the Mess Steward and shown to his room, which he was to share with another of his course members who had yet to arrive.

He had about an hour in which to change into his mess dress before dinner and was settling himself into what he hoped would be his home for the next fourteen weeks, provided he 'stayed the course,' when his new roommate was ushered in. "Alex Shooter" he said extending his hand to shake that of the newcomer. "Ken King" replied the newcomer politely taking Alex's proffered hand. Alex said, "I've grabbed the bed against the inside wall I'm afraid, yours is by the window. Still with a decent fire we should both be snug enough in here." Bathed and suitably attired Alex set off for the bar leaving Ken to follow once he was ready. Ten minutes before dinner the fifteen Officers of the new intake of Trainee Pilots were making themselves known to each other and swapping stories of their service experiences. Alex noted that Ken was a man of some stature being both tall, over six feet, and barrel-chested. He was also rather quiet and introspective, which for a Gunner was somewhat rare.

The following morning they were roused from their beds at 0600 hours by a Batman knocking on their door and bringing in two steaming mugs of tea. "Breakfast in half an hour gentleman, and new intake to parade on the drive, in battledress, at 0715 hours," said the Batty cheerfully as he smoothly made his way out, before noisily closing the door just make sure that his charges were not slipping back into their slumbers.

An assorted bag of young Artillery Officers was milling about outside the front door of the Manor House shortly after seven a.m. most of them building upon the introductions made in the Mess after dinner on the previous night when an immaculately turned-out Royal Air Force Warrant Officer briskly marched up to them. He held his Pace Stick firmly under his left armpit, ruler straight and parallel with the ground. This slightly built and rather diminutive figure all of five feet six inches tall, but full of military bull and correctness, stamped to a halt and bellowed in a deep voice totally out of keeping with his stature "Gentlemen." He paused and scrutinized the assembled Artillery Officers before continuing with a voice that would have awakened the dead. "I presume that you are the new intake for the EFTS." Another pause during which a few of the would-be Pilots responded "yes, we are." Some were heard to say "Sergeant Major," and a cheery lone voice with "Warrant." The Warrant Officer, Class One, went a rare shade of puce. He took several deep breaths before speaking very firmly, initially relatively quietly then gradually increasing in volume, addressed them again. "I am not a bleedin' Sarn't Major, I am a Warrant Officer in His Majesty's Royal Air Force." His face contorted and he bellowed louder than ever, "I am not a 'Warrant' either: address me as that again and you will have a Warrant pushed where the sun don't shine, and you will be using it as your authority to travel to most remote bleedin' Pongo Camp I can think of!" Another very pregnant pause followed by an ear shattering "do I make myself clear. Gentlemen." After another short pause he continued with slightly less force to his voice "now get fell in three ranks, if as Trainee Officer Pilots you can recall the basic drill that some poor sod of a Drill Sergeant must have tried to knock into you." The rather subdued group quickly arranged themselves into five files of three ranks standing to attention, shuffling slightly to attain some semblance of order and 'right dress'.

The Warrant Officer again looked them over with a slightly disdainful eye before addressing them in a softer and more reasonable tone. "I am not here to teach you drill, or how to be soldiers, or even airmen. However, I am here to make sure that you learn, and to do so very quickly, the differences between the ways of the Royal Air Force and the Army. I am the Station Warrant Officer at RAF Cambridge and as such I have responsibility to the Station Commander for both discipline and the smooth running of the Station. You will hear me referred to the 'ess double-you oh or swoh,' and sometimes by other less savoury titles." He paused for chuckles of which there were none, although several smiles broke out on the Officers' faces. "You will address me as Mister Grimmer" a statement that elicited even bigger grins on the faces of those standing before him. "Yes, I know, I've heard all the jokes before. 'Grim reaper, Happy Harry and so on."

A bus painted in Air Force blue had drawn up, facing down the drive, some yards away. Mister Grimmer pointed towards the bus and stated, "that gentlemen, is your transport between here and the aerodrome. It's not a Raff bus, it is the property of the King for the use of members of the ahr ay eff" he paused then continued "not the raff: raff and riff go hand in hand, and we are not riff-raff." With that he snapped smartly to attention and barked out the order, "Squaaad: squad, … attennn'shun. Squaaad, to your duties diiiisssmisss." With that, he smartly turned to his right, saluted, and marched off to the bus, as did the assembled course members.

Chapter 6

Ab-initio Training

The pre-war Airport had been privately owned by the well-established Marshall family. Marshalls of Cambridge was a totally family-owned local engineering and aeronautical business which had also provided basic flying training to civilians and the RAF until the outbreak of the war. The new Civic Airport had opened in nineteen thirty-eight. It was situated on the eastern side of the city to the south of the Newmarket Road and to the immediate west of the village of Teversham. With outbreak of the War Marshall's Civic Airport had come under the control of the Royal Air Force and designated RAF Cambridge. The fleet of Tiger Moth aircraft owned by Marshall's Flying School, and the Cambridge Aero Club, were placed under the control of 22 Elementary Flying Training School which had been providing ab-initio training to Military Pilots pre-war under Marshall's contract with the Air Ministry. It was at the offices of 22 EFTS located in the former terminal building, which had been designed by a local University of Cambridge architect in nineteen thirty-seven, that the fifteen aspiring Army Pilots were introduced to their Flight Commanders and Instructors.

The regime at the Training School was unrelenting, there was little time to slope off into the city for a night out, with a syllabus that required one hundred hours of formal classroom based ground school leading to stringent tests on each of the subject areas. Quite a degree of self-study was also required to gain the required levels of knowledge necessary to pass the written examinations. The winter days were relatively short and the weather was often appalling, totally unfit for flying training. Some of the ground school subjects had to be mastered before their actual flying lessons could begin. Other tests were 'make or break' for the students if they were to progress or, in the event of failure, be returned to their Parent Unit if deemed to be unsuited to flying duties. They started with the theory of flight learning about lift, weight, thrust, and drag as the principal forces that affected the airframe in flight. Then onto how lift is generated by the shape of the wing section and the angle of attack, the angle of the airflow meeting the leading edge of the wing relative to the wing section, and the different types of wing section applicable to aircraft performance requirements. They learned about airframes and undercarriages, engines including the fuel, air and exhaust systems, cockpit instruments relating to the performance of both engine and aircraft, as well as both high and very high frequency radio sets.

Their lessons were not designed to turn them into Airframe Fitters or Riggers, Engine Mechanics, or Radio Technicians. However, they had to know enough to be able to recognise when things were not working as they should and to have sufficient skill to fix minor faults quickly whilst away from the support of the Ground Staff at their home bases. The knowledge and skills gained were essential for them to carry out the necessary pre-flight inspections that would be required of them as Captains of the aircraft that they would be flying on a daily basis. They knew that that the Ground Staff, in RAF terms 'erks,' would have prepared the aircraft for operational use. Nevertheless, they were ultimately responsible for the aircraft and its safety in operational use.

They were immersed in practical radio work, the phonetic alphabet and the use of codes applicable to aerodrome operations as well as those more generally applicable in the battle zones over which they would be flying once they had gained their 'wings' and passed the even more demanding operational training, and aircraft conversion, courses that would follow. In that section of the syllabus they also had to get to grips with the 'Rules of the Air' and the various ground to air and air to ground signals that were used to ensure, as far as possible, the safe conduct of flying operations at 'regular' aerodromes and 'satellite' landing grounds. Alex loved every minute of the ground school and soaked up the information like a sponge. He gained high marks in all the tests as his training progressed. He developed a deep interest in meteorology and spent much of his notionally free time poring over the met charts in the Pilot's briefing rooms at the airport. He befriended the Meteorological Officers and learned more from them as they put together the forecasts that would be used for briefing the aircrews. His knowledge of the Atlantic weather charts allowed him to determine whether or not the following day, or days, would be suitable for flying before the daily orders were posted and the students briefed for the day's work schedule.

Then there was the flying. Alex couldn't wait to get airborne in the de Havilland Tiger Moths that were the basic training machines used by 22 Elementary Flying Training School. These light aeroplanes were relatively docile and excellent machines for training ab-initio Pilots. They were quite responsive to the Pilot's inputs. The flying controls were not particularly well harmonised, and to achieve a smoothly executed banked turn the Pilot had to apply rudder in the direction of the turn slightly before banking the aircraft. However, they needed constant vigilance to fly them well. It was said that if one could fly a de Havilland Tiger Moth safely one was a Pilot, if one could fly a Tiger Moth well one was an exceptional Pilot, and if one could regularly land it as smoothly as if applying butter to soft bread one was an extraordinarily gifted Pilot. Alex very quickly proved that he was going to be an exceptional, and possibly a gifted, Pilot. After only five and a half hours of dual instruction he was sent off on his first solo flight. He was briefed to take off, fly one circuit of the airfield, and land. It was impressed upon him that he was to remain in the circuit of the former Civic Airport. He was not to overfly either the City or the Village and in the event of an engine failure on take-off he was to land straight ahead. His circuit was flown faultlessly, and he touched down on three points without a hint of a bounce, his previous experience as a glider Pilot played a great part in that almost unheard-of achievement.

The first Student Pilot to leave the course was an eager young Officer who was found to suffer from aggressive allergic rhinitis, hay fever. The hapless young man had managed, somehow or another, to disguise this fact at his medical examination in his keenness to serve as a Pilot. He was rapidly posted to desk job in a Staff Appointment at the War Office. One of the other fourteen Student Pilots failed to reach the standard of aircraft handling necessary to be sent solo; he was washed out of training and returned to his Regiment. As the course progressed a further two Trainees were returned to their Regiments having failed the navigation tests. There was the usual crop of accidents. One unfortunate Student Pilot misjudged his approach to landing and dropped his tired aircraft in an unduly nose high attitude, from several feet up, onto the grass runway tail skid first. The skid dug in abruptly slowing the machine which crashed down onto the main wheels collapsing the undercarriage. The Tyro crawled from the wreckage shaking himself like a dog emerging from water with blood streaming down his face from a broken nose and gash on his forehead. He was sent to hospital to recover and was allowed to continue training on the next course available.

The remaining ten Student Pilots passed their grading tests with bland 'satisfactory' endorsements in their logbooks. The Commanding Officer of 22 EFTS further endorsed Alex's logbook with a green entry stating 'exceptional.' The party that Friday evening in the Mess was also more than usually rowdy, high spirited and eventually quite drunken. Sore heads, alleviated to a degree by long draws from aircraft oxygen bottles, were much in evidence the following morning. Mister Grimmer had them on parade at 0800 hours, they looked the worse for wear and the SWO told them so in no uncertain terms. Wilting under his stare and grimacing at the pains in their heads as he bawled his comments about their fitness to be Pilots, they stoically stood their ground in three ranks with one blank file. Having had his formal say, he stood them at ease and then gave a stand easy command. A big smile broke out on his face as he surveyed them for some seconds: then quiet gently he said "gentlemen, congratulations! You have been a pleasure to have under my supervision and are a credit to your Regiments. Not only have you gained your wings, which will be presented by the Station Commander this afternoon, but you have acquitted yourselves in fine style when in and around the station and in the city. Despite the drunken orgy you enjoyed last night, but doubtless cannot remember, you have shown the stamina and professionalism required to appear on parade this morning and even look like the Officers and Gentlemen I know you to be." "Your postings will be placed on the notice board at 1700 hours this afternoon. Good luck to you all." After another quite long pause he bellowed "Squaaaad," they all braced up, "squad, ahh – ten – shun." As one the squad of newly fledged Pilots snapped to attention basking in the complimentary words that had been spoken. "Squad, to your duties: diss – miss." Smart right turns and crisp salutes completed, they broke ranks into an informal knot of chums who 'bimbled' off to the mess to prepare for their wings parade. As the SWO marched proudly away, one of the now very sober Pilots said "knock me down with a feather duster, the 'grim reaper' is human after all!"

Chapter 7

Operational training

Exactly at 1700 hours the Orderly Room 'erk' pinned a notice on the board in the Junior Officer's Mess. With more than a little jostling the newly qualified Army Pilots eagerly scanned the Orders. All were posted back to their parent Regiments pending the commencement of the next Operational Training Course. The course would be provided by D Flight 43 Operational Training Unit RAF, based at Old Sarum. This airfield was located close to Salisbury in Wiltshire and promised to be a good station on the edge of the Salisbury Plain training area. Released from duties the following day, Saturday, they made their way into Cambridge to celebrate their good fortune of being posted en-mass to face the rigours of operational training.

Alex had managed to contact Jane Squires within a day or two of his first arrival at Stow-cum-Quy and in his few, and far between, off duty hours they had spent time together catching up on their activities since they had been together at the last Summer Ball of Alex and Ollie's time at Oakham in nineteen thirty-seven. She had invited him, together with all his fellow Student Pilots, to a dance in Hall at Newnham College. Newnham College was a female only undergraduate college within the University. As eligible young bachelor Officers and Gentlemen they were made very welcome by the young ladies looking for dance partners that evening. Alex spent much of the evening with Jane. She was disappointed to learn that he would be posted away so soon but the bond was established, and at the end of the evening they promised to write and visit together whenever opportunities arose during the following weeks. Romance started to blossom, and the two spent as much time together as they could manage within the limitations imposed by their respective schedules.

Seven days leave was granted to each of the course members upon its completion. Alex chose to stay in Cambridge for the greater part of the week in which his feelings for Jane became serious enough for them to be thinking about their future relationship, despite it having been somewhat of a whirlwind romance. He could not justify the petrol needed to drive to his parent's home. So it was that he left his little car with Jane in Cambridge as he bade her a fond farewell, which included an almost shy suggestion that they might consider marriage, at the town's railway station. Jane smiled broadly, threw her arms around his neck hugging him to her and kissed him passionately in response. It was hard for him to take his departure that Thursday afternoon for a fleeting visit with his parents near Selkirk in the Scottish Borders. His mother was overjoyed to see her son after such a long period of absence but she was also troubled that he had opted for a life of danger as a Pilot; her spoken view being "if God had intended man to fly, he would have given us angels' wings". She was reputed to be somewhat fey and her unease at Alexander's flying career was in part due to dark premonitions of the future. Perhaps her unease about flying over-rode any indications as to her feelings regarding her son's romantic attachment and marital plans since, although touched upon, they were never raised in any serious conversation between Alex and his parents.

He was due to report to 43 Operational Training Unit at RAF Old Sarum at 0800 hours on Monday the fourth of May nineteen forty-two, thus he reluctantly took his leave of his parents on the Sunday morning. Early on that morning, armed with a pack of food to a travel warrant for the train journey south and west, he bade them a fond farewell. He arrived at Salisbury railway station shortly after 0600 hours on the Monday morning. An Austin one-and-a-half-ton truck was waiting to take him and several others to their temporary quarters at Salisbury Manor. This was to be a short stay lasting but a few days whilst administrative matters plus an introduction to the Ground School topics were given strict attention: these were presented in some detail respectively. The working day was hectic; however, the evenings were relaxed and spent investigating the delights of Salisbury.

Jane had delivered his car to him shortly after his posting to D Flight and they had enjoyed a few hours together in which they further pledged themselves to each other pending a formal engagement. She made her way home by train from Salisbury to Thrapston Midland Station; that journey had proven to be something of a nightmare with innumerable hold-ups and changes of train. The journey had taken just over sixteen hours all told having been interrupted by an air raid on London whilst she was making her way from Waterloo to St Pancras on the Underground, which had stopped running whilst the raid was in progress and the stations were used as air raid shelters.

Alex had maintained a regular correspondence with Jane throughout his Operational Training Course. She had by then completed her course at Cambridge University, with excellent examination grades, but being a woman was not allowed to receive a Degree from the University. She had temporarily returned to her parent's home in the historic market town of Thrapston in Northamptonshire. She was desperate to find something useful to occupy her time but also wanted to be with Alex as much as possible.

New orders had the latest course members moving to hutted accommodation at Larkhill, an Army Camp on the edge of Salisbury Plain, close to Stonehenge. The winter weather made Larkhill a miserable spot and the wooden huts were draughty. The sole means of heating was a coal fired, pot-bellied, cast-iron stove which was mounted on a stone slab in the centre of each hut. The chimney flue, some six inches in diameter, rose vertically from the rear of the stove and out through the roof. A single bucket of coal and kindling material was provided to each hut on a daily basis.

When Alex arrived at Larkhill D Flight had a very mixed bag of aircraft comprising a single Taylorcraft Plus D also known as an Auster Mk I, several Piper Cubs, a Stinson Reliant, a de Havilland Tiger Moth, and an ancient Avro Tutor. It was rumoured that the newer Taylorcraft Auster Mk III aircraft were entering service and that D flight would have at least one of these allocated before the New Year.

It was at Larkhill, and over the open spaces of the Salisbury Plain training area, that the newly fledged Pilots got to grips with the demands of operational flying. The course was crammed into a mere two months during which there was no let up from the pressure of mastering the new skills required in so short a time. Great emphasis was placed on aircraft handling, especially operation at minimum level, hedge hopping. It was essential that the Pilots should be able to fly instinctively since in the air observation role the risk of mental overload could spell disaster.

A much more demanding and nerve-wracking part of the advanced flying training that had to be fully mastered was that of flight by sole reference to the instruments, and operating the aircraft in bad weather with very restricted visibility. The layouts of the instrument panels of the different aircraft available to the Tyro Pilots were not standardised, and the Pilot had to become familiar with these individual layouts. They had to develop a scanning technique to check the information presented by each instrument in turn to avoid fixation on one particular source. During periods when flying was not scheduled, or they were grounded due to appallingly bad weather, Alex and his chums sat in the cockpits of the various aircraft learning to identify the various switches and instruments by touch alone, eyes tightly closed. Their Instructors drumming into them that in the heat of action they must not lose their focus whilst looking, or fumbling, for switches.

Similarly, they practiced scanning the Performance and Attitude Instruments as if in flight in zero visibility. The Performance Instrument Group were the Airspeed Indicator, the Altimeter, and the Vertical Speed Indicator; the Attitude Group comprised the Turn and Slip Indicator, the Level Indicator, or Artificial Horizon if one was fitted, and the Compass together with the Direction Indicator when one was fitted. The Pilots also had to keep an eye on the Engine Instruments which were the Rev-counter, Oil Temperature and Pressure Gauges, Cylinder Head Temperature gauge, and Fuel Gaug.

Supplementing their time in the aircraft they were also required to spend time in a somewhat basic simulator, the 'Link Trainer' which provided the Trainee with an enclosed cockpit mounted on a system of levers, with pumps, valves, and bellows that would respond to the Pilot's control column and rudder pedal inputs as if in flight. The whole contraption including the instruments was linked, by an electro-pneumatic and mechanical system to a plotting table on which the pattern of the 'flight' was drawn out on a chart.

Operationally, acting in support of artillery, Pilots were often required to land in fields close to the guns or Armoured Unit Headquarters. Since the landing areas were not prepared landing grounds the course members were taught the art of field evaluation and short field landings; the latter being important to reduce the risk of damage to the aircraft should there be any hazards that might be hidden in the grass, or crop, on the landing run. The basics of field selection had been covered in the ab-initio training under the heading of precautionary landings and forced landings without power. As part of the field evaluation exercises the Pilots were also tasked to seek out suitable fields which could be quickly developed as Advanced Landing Grounds, ALG's. Alex quickly acquired the knack of getting his aircraft down in the smallest of fields and more importantly how to get his machine out again safely. He had an acute sense of what is sometimes referred to as situational awareness and could 'sniff out' fields that were suitable and reject those that 'just didn't feel right.' He revelled in low level operations and flying his aircraft to the limits of the flight envelope from the unaccelerated stall to the maximum safe manoeuvring speed and the maximum speed that the aircraft could achieve in a dive without sustaining damage. His flight commander quickly recognised that Alex was both an exceptional Pilot and, even more importantly, one who was particularly good at assisting his fellow course members to succeed.

Individual Flights of the Squadrons would operate from makeshift airfields and be served by a ground contingent of RAF Aircraftmen with either an Officer or Senior NCO to command them. These unsung heroes worked tirelessly to provide for the physical needs of the Aircrews and the operational efficiency of the Flights. There were Engine and Airframe fitters, Radio and Camera Technicians, Refuelling Teams, Firefighters, as well as the Field Kitchen Crews and Mobile Bath Units. Administration Teams, who kept the paperwork flowing, to ensure that records were kept and spares, parts, and every other thing that the was needed to support the Aircrews in their tasks were also supplied by the RAF. Officially the Pilots remained as members of their 'parent' Regiments.

As a Battery Officer Alex had been well respected as an able Gunner who was quick getting into action and had a first-class brain capable of dealing with the complex mathematics of ballistics. This was of particular value to an AOP Pilot who had the learn to judge the flight of the shells, from the guns with which he was working, to a tight margin. Directing the guns was Alex's favourite activity; it required the skills of low flying and accurate navigation to ensure that the aircraft was in the right place at the right time to 'call the shots' and then be correctly placed to register the 'fall of shot' and issue corrections to the Gunners whilst getting back down 'in the weeds' before the enemy could fire at the spotter aircraft.

The Instructional Staff recognised that it was partially due to Alex's patient and confident manner whilst coaching his fellow tyros that there were no 'washouts' from his course. Nearly all the Pilots that had successfully completed their operational training were allocated to the Air Observation Post Squadrons as operational Pilots. However, not all were posted immediately and remained with D Flight pending posting. So it was that on Friday the eleventh of August nineteen forty-two that Lt. Colonel John Merton RE, the Commanding Officer of D Flight, sent for Alex and asked him if would undertake a Course of Instruction to qualify as an Instructor, and remain with D Flight, instead of being posted to a new AOP Squadron that was to be formed at Old Sarum. Alex readily accepted the invitation recognising that it would provide the degree of stability in his life that he felt was necessary to start his life with Jane as his wife. He had no illusions about the future. He recognised that an Operational Posting would eventually place him in harm's way. However, he could not envisage that he would be taken from the important task of building up the strength of the Air Observation Post Squadrons until a major operation was in the offing to take the war back to the battlefields on the Continent. When Alex wrote to tell Jane about his posting to D Flight's Instructional Staff they both felt that the relative security, and stability, of the posting was a heaven-sent opportunity to announce their engagement to be married. Both families very much approved of their plans and were tremendously supportive. Jane's brother Ollie, who had followed Alex's promptings and was in training as a prospective AOP Pilot at 8 EFTS based at RAF Woodley near Reading in Berkshire, was overjoyed at the news.

They took such opportunities as presented when Alex had twenty-four hour passes to meet; although civilian travel to Salisbury was difficult for Jane. Despite the difficulties their relationship grew ever closer and warmer to the degree that their proposed marriage was very much to the forefront of their minds. Arrangements were made for Jane to move to Salisbury as soon as possible. She was still determined to play her part in the war effort and decided that she would apply to join the First Aid Nursing Yeomanry as soon as she was settled in her new home, wherever that might be. For both Alex and Jane planning the arrangements for their Wedding Day was at the forefront of their minds, finding a home together wasn't their highest priority. Whether the wedding would be held in Jane's family hometown of Thrapston in Northamptonshire or somewhere around Salisbury or at whichever Army Camp to which Alex was posted was the most difficult part of their planning. No matter where the ceremony was to be held it was evident that travel from Selkirk to the venue would be a challenge for Alex's parents. Nevertheless, they were determined that they would find a way to be present and to share their love with Alex's new bride to be. In the event Jane's parents partially solved the problem by inviting Alex's parents to stay with them for several days so that there would be less pressure for the Shooters with both travel and accommodation arrangements. So it was that the wedding plans were finalised. Once Alex had obtained the agreement of his Commanding Officer to the plans for the proposed wedding he was assured that he would be granted seven days leave. The Parish Priest at St James' Church in Thrapston was duly approached with a request for Miss Jane Anne Squires, Spinster of that Parish, be married to Lieutenant Alexander James Shooter MC RA on Saturday the first day of May Nineteen forty-three. The banns were posted and the preparations went ahead without a hitch. The Bridge Hotel was booked for the Reception and a Hotel at a destination kept secret from all and sundry was booked for the Honeymoon by Alex and Jane. The letter of confirmation for their booking was the first that they received addressed to Lt. and Mrs Shooter, a fact that made them smile with a mutual feeling of deep togetherness.

Chapter 8

Posting

All too soon the Honeymoon was over and Alex had to report to his CO at RAF Old Sarum, Salisbury, at 0700 hours on the morning of Friday the seventh of May nineteen forty-three to resume his duties as an Instructor with D flight. His CO told him not to get too comfortable in his billet since there were postings in the wind. Alex was told that with the Americans joining the war in Europe there would be a need for them to be trained to work with their Allies. It was also thought that the American Pilots, and Observers, flying Liaison and Ground Attack Aircraft would have to be trained to operate in the skies over European terrain in the weather typically encountered over Western Europe. His CO went on to say that as far as he was concerned Alex was ideally suited, both in his training abilities and personality, to get along with the Yanks when they showed up. Alex assured his CO that, if the opportunity arose, he would be first in line to volunteer for the role. He saw it as another opportunity for adventure and developing new skills.

On Sunday the fifth of September Alex was the Duty Officer going through the Daily Orders to be posted that morning when he spotted an entry which read "Officers wishing to volunteer for service on detachment to the United States of America's Army Air Force must apply, in writing, to their immediate Superior Officer." All other considerations forgotten, Alex immediately wrote a letter of application to his CO. The wheels of bureaucracy ground slowly and three weeks passed without any indication of whether or not his application for detached duty had been accepted. Alex was fretting and eager to be off with a new challenge in front of him. On Monday the twenty-seventh of September he saw the CO coming his way, "I've got to ask him about that job with the Yanks" he said to himself. He threw up a smart salute as his CO stopped in front of him: before he could open his mouth, he heard "you had better get your kit packed and your desk tidied away Shooter. I have it on very good authority that you are about to be posted to a place called RAF Upham Manor somewhere in West Sussex. Good luck, I think that you are going to need it. Oh! And congratulations you are being Gazetted Captain with effect from today's date." The orders posting Captain A J Shooter MC to RAF Upham Manor on detached duty to the USAAF were posted in the Daily Orders on the following Sunday.

On Monday morning the fourth of October nineteen forty-three Alex drove down to West Sussex in his little Austin seven car where he reported to the Duty Officer at the main gate guard post of RAF Upham Manor, West Sussex. The duty Guard Commander, a young American Second Lieutenant, looked puzzled and stated in very formal tones "sir, you will have to wait here. I have no orders to permit any non-US personnel to access the Base." Alex replied, "You should have been notified of my posting to RAF Upham Manor as a Liaison Officer, here are my written orders and my identity documents." He handed the Guard Commander his papers. The young American looked at the papers in his hand before saying "sir, unless authorised by the Base Commander I cannot permit you to enter the Base. You will remain here under guard until I receive confirmation of posting: sir." With that he turned on his heel and marched into the wooden hut that passed for the Guardroom, whilst so doing he ordered the Guard at the gate to detain the Britisher right there. It wasn't the wisest of orders since Alex's car was parked in front of the barrier, in the middle of the road, blocking all traffic both in and outbound.

Five minutes elapsed before a Jeep, that had come racing from behind some buildings to the left of the airfield, slid to a halt beside the Guardroom. A very annoyed looking British Squadron Leader and a red-faced American Major jumped out of the Jeep. The Squadron Leader stepped quickly over to Alex with his right hand extended in greeting. He said "sorry for the upset old boy the paperwork telling us of your posting has been sitting on the Base Commander's desk over the weekend, and he's away at some meeting or other until tomorrow. His deputy, Major Wendell here, has only just found it. Welcome to RAF Upham Manor, I'm Archie Cross the nominal Stationmaster here, although for all practical purposes it operates as part of the US Army Air Force under the Command of Lieutenant Colonel Gene Monson. I do hope that your time here will prove to be more pleasant than your introduction might have indicated." Major Wendell stepped up to Alex. Alex threw up a salute to recognise his superior Officer. The Major smiled, the redness was dissipating from his face and neck, as he extended his hand to shake Alex's. "Sure glad to have you come over to us Cap'n Shooter. Say, that's a swell name for fighting man. I'm sure that we can get along real well once we get to know each other." With that he stomped into the Guardroom where he loudly assured the Guard Commander that he had done a great job, and that the Limey Captain was one of the good guys who would be saying at the base a while.

The American Training Scheme for familiarisation with British, Commonwealth and other Allied forces had hardly been tested when Alex arrived at Upham Manor. As the only British Artillery Officer at the Airbase it fell to him to work out a scheme of classroom training and operational conversion flying for his American charges. It required a delicacy of touch to bring the gung-ho American Pilots to accept the need for any familiarisation flying in the first place. Also, for them to accept that they were going to be operating, at least for part of their time, under British Army Orders. He gently pointed out that both he and they were going to have to learn each other's codes, orders, and phonetic alphabets if they were to avoid the most awful 'cock-ups' in battle. He made it quite clear to them that European geography and weather were a lot different from what they were used to flying over and through in the States. Also, the airspace over England was very busy and the airfield movement control orders were different from those used at their training airfields in the USA. To make the point, and hopefully to gain some leverage, he offered to take the American Flight Commanders for familiarisation flights in aircraft fitted with dual controls. This had a two-fold purpose since he needed to become familiar with as many of the aircraft being operated by the USAAF at Upham Manor as possible in very short order as well as demonstrating his point about the differences between the American and British regimes.

The Liaison airplanes, as his American friends called them, were small machines not dissimilar to the Taylorcraft - Auster marques with which the British AOP Squadrons were equipped. The American Piper L4 'Grasshopper' model was a development of an original design, by the English engineer C G Taylor, which had been taken up by William T Piper in nineteen thirty. They also had Aeronca L3 airplanes, also nicknamed 'Grasshoppers,' which again had similar flying characteristics to the Piper L4 and Auster marques. The principal difference between the British and American machines was that the British Austers had wider fuselages allowing for side-by-side seating and a rearward facing observer's seat behind the right-hand front seat. The American machines had narrower fuselages with tandem seating arrangements for only two crew. The USAAF also had a flight of A7 'Apache' Ground Attack aircraft based at Upham Manor: these thoroughbreds came from the same stable as the mighty P51 Mustang fighter. It was the job of the British Instructors at RAF Upham Manor to ensure the Pilots of these single seat fighter bombers could operate safely, and effectively, with their Allies. Alex longed for an opportunity to take to the skies in one of these wild horses, but he wasn't given the chance before they moved elsewhere.

The workload was demanding at first; Alex had so much to do in a very short period of time. Nevertheless, by mid-October when he had been joined by two other former D Flight Instructors he had the training schedules sorted out. The Ground School course structure was complete, together with the lesson notes and the necessary Army and RAF Memoranda available for issue to the American student Pilots and Observers. He had also won over the Americans such that they accepted him as one of their own. He had achieved this partly by being at the top of his game and partly by joining in with their social life; he proved to be an excellent baseball pitcher and was also fairly good with a bat.

Social life also extended to Alex and his fellow Instructors taking their chums to the local pubs: one of Alex favourites was the Old White Hart Inn in Upham village. When first posted to RAF Upham Manor he had lived in the Officers' Quarters on the base. However, both he and Jane wanted to be together as much as possible, especially when off duty and out at the pub, so they looked to set up a home together as close to the Airbase as possible. They found a delightful cottage in the nearby village of Middle Down with which they fell in love from the moment they first saw it. They spoke to their respective parents about buying the cottage, asking if they could help to raise the money to buy it outright. Both sets of parents agreed to provide the necessary funding on a fifty-fifty basis making up the balance of the purchase price from that which Alex and Jane had been able to put aside since their engagement. They moved into their sparsely furnished 'love nest' on Saturday the first of January nineteen forty-four. They agreed that they didn't need much furniture other than a comfortable bed, a kitchen table and a couple of kitchen chairs, a pair of armchairs and a sofa would suffice to begin with. Friends and family made sure that they had enough to be comfortable, and to feel secure in their own home.

The training eventually had the American Liaison crews flying to sites many miles from their base in West Sussex. Their training took them to places in Wales, Scotland, North Yorkshire, Cumbria, Dorset, and Cornwall where they would participate in various British, American and then Combined Operations exercises, including operating with both British Royal and American Navy ships directing naval gunfire.

The Spring of nineteen forty-four saw the whole of southern England becoming an armed camp: it was evident to almost everyone that these massed forces were being assembled in readiness for a major offensive. The American Army Air Force training units no longer required the presence of British Army and Royal Air Force Instructors to prepare new aircrew for combined operations in the European Theatre. RAF Upham Manor's USAAF teams were more than capable of running the training schemes required. The British Instructors were posted back to D Flight at Old Sarum with effect from Saturday the twenty fifth of

March nineteen forty-four. Alex applied for, and was granted, a week of annual leave which he spent quietly with Jane in their beautiful little cottage on Church Lane in Middle Down. The Americans at Upham Down would not let their British 'buddies' go without a 'really swell party'. The party was started off in the mess hall by Colonel Gene Monson who formally thanked Alex and his team for their hard work and dedication in keeping his wild boys alive during training and giving them the confidence, born of real experience, to operate in European skies with the Allies. Squadron Leader Archie Cross added a few well-chosen words praising his army colleagues and wishing them well for the future. After the formalities came the fun which was started by the American Trainees hoisting their British Instructors shoulder high and parading them around their Air Base to the cheers and applause of the ground crews and administration staff. They were then taken back to the mess hall for a farewell dinner. The evening was rounded off at the Old White Hart in Upham village where the beers and such spirits that were to be had flowed until the early hours of the morning. Charlie Fowler, the Landlord had warned the local Police Constable that there was to be a private party at the inn, at which he would be a welcome guest. Many tales were recounted, some funny, some serious, but all related to fond memories of the time that the British Instructors had spent with their American hosts; at one point one of the British group, rather loudly pointed out the Americans were the visitors to good old England, but this was taken in good part with gales of laughter and toasts to 'good old England' and the 'land of the free'. The base transport section drivers made sure that everyone got home safely, even though most were a bit 'worse for wear!'

On Friday the thirty first of March nineteen forty-four Captain A J Shooter reported to the Officer of the Day at the gates of RAF Old

Sarum. He was told that he wasn't expected but if he cared to 'warn in' at Officer's Mess the Mess Steward would make provision for him. Alex had a leisurely morning doing the rounds of the hangars and offices where he learned that the latest versions of the Auster AOP marks were soon to be brought into service. The Mark IV's were already in service with some of the Squadrons and the Mark V's would be issued within a matter of weeks. Both marks had air-cooled American Lycoming engines, these had a flat four, horizontally opposed, piston arrangement and developed one hundred and thirty horsepower. The earlier marks of the Auster AOP series had four cylinder in-line air-cooled engines and were lighter than the newer Marks IV and V. The Lycoming flat four engines were shorter, but broader, than the in-line engines but gave the Pilot a slighter better view ahead when on the ground. The newer marks were also fitted with split flaps which had three stages. The first stage provided an increase in the lift generated by the wing, without a significant increase in drag, this allowed for a shorter take-off run and a steeper climb away. The intermediate stage increased both the lift and drag produced by the airflow over the wing which allowed for a lower nose attitude in the early stages of approach to landing and reduced the stalling speed of the aircraft. The fully deployed stage of flap increased both the lift and drag still further. This third stage, full flap, setting reduced the stalling speed even more and allowed a more significant nose down attitude to be adopted during the final approach to landing. This greatly improved the Pilot's view of the runway and with the lower stalling speed the landing distance required was significantly reduced. These innovations made operations from small airstrips surrounded by trees more viable. The Auster AOP Mark V aircraft were also equipped for night flying and had fittings to allow for the mounting of armour plate beneath the Pilot's seat.

Chapter 9

Into Action

Alex was held at Old Sarum for a fortnight as supernumerary Pilot before a posting to 659 Squadron, which had moved south from Clifton near York on the twenty third of April nineteen forty-four to operate from East Grinstead, a small Landing Ground, located approximately seven and a half miles east of RAF Gatwick came through. There were rumours that 659 were going to be moved again and would be based at Old Sarum pending allocation to the Army Group with which they would operate. Early in May the Squadron's Commanding Officer told the married men that he would do all that he could to arrange for forty-eight and seventy-two hour passes to be granted to them before the end of the month. Alex was over the Moon when he got a forty-eight for the thirteenth and fourteenth of the month. He drove home in his trusty Austin Seven car for a quiet weekend with his beloved wife. As the invasion of Hitler's Fortress Europe drew close in the first few days of June, the Squadron's Headquarters was moved to Old Sarum, and was assigned to work with units of the Twenty-first Army Group. In the days immediately following D-Day Alex was kept busy at the Squadron HQ with the logistics of moving the Squadron's aircraft and ground support organisation to their assigned Advanced Landing Ground, designated B6, near Cully in Normandy some four miles into the bridgehead behind the eastern end of Gold beach.

Alex was given command of the Advance Party and was sent to prepare the landing ground for the arrival of the Squadron, and to ensure that the aircraft would be ready for action as quickly as possible. He, together with a Junior Officer as his Observer, was allocated a brand-new Auster AOP Mark V with the serial number TW348 to cross the Channel and 'set up shop' on ALG B6, which was still under construction, close to the villages of Sainte-Croix-sur-Mer and Cully. The Squadron was declared operational on the fourteenth of June nineteen forty-four at ALG B6. Individual Flights were tasked as required; which often meant that their aircraft would operate away from their base, landing and taking off from other Advanced Landing Grounds and even from unprepared fields close to the Gun Batteries with which they were tasked to work. They had hardly set up their Operations Base at B6 when the Squadron was ordered, on the twenty third of June, to move to ALG B9 at Lantheuil approximately one and half miles to the southeast. Whilst at Lantheuil the Squadron started to receive the rest of the brand-new Auster AOP Mark V aircraft which were allocated to them. The Squadron HQ was never anywhere for very long. In mid-July they moved to ALG B12 near Basly. Two days later another relocation a mile away to Beny-sur-mer. Then after a further ten days to ALG B31 close to Noron-de-Poterie, which lay five miles to the southwest of Bayeaux. This move was a logistical nightmare for the Squadron HQ team. The road contingent had to move across the front through the supply lines from the Beaches, and the Mulberry harbour at Arromanches, to the front lines causing chaos, and considerable frustration to the Military Police who were posted at key road junctions tasked with ensuring the smooth flow of traffic to the front. All the while the Flights were operating into and from Landing Grounds within the Normandy Beachhead, some of which were quite makeshift and had no prepared runways. They refuelled their aircraft, by hand, from both two-gallon petrol tins and the newly adopted 'Jerry' cans that were brought up their fields in the supply echelon vehicles. These carried mixed loads including food, fuel, and ammunition. The Drivers of these vehicles were doing dangerous work and putting in long hours, moving mainly between dusk and dawn to avoid being spotted and shelled by the enemy artillery. Alex, and the other aircrew, did what they could to take care of the echelon drivers, recognising their essential role and the demands that were placed upon them.

The Squadron was operational at their new location by the thirtieth of July and providing support to the troops involved in Operation Bluecoat acting as the Left-flank Guard to the American Operation Cobra which was aimed at punching through the enemy line to take the port of Avranches and isolating the German forces in the Cotentin Peninsular. As the Allies pushed southwest towards the town of Vire the Squadron followed the Eleventh Armoured Division's leading elements with a move first to ALG B39 in the neighbourhood of La Fouquerie; then five days later on the seventh of August they were sent couple of miles southeast to ALG B40, at La Terrierre. During this move Alex had been dispatched to provide fire control for a shoot against 88mm anti-tank gun positions that were holding up the advance of the Third Division troops and their supporting armour. Alex completed his shoot and landed near the Eighth Army Group Royal Artillery HQ close to the small town of Le Beny Bocage to report intelligence he had gathered post action. Whilst making his report an urgent call came in from the Eleventh Armoured Divisional

HQ. Their Reconnaissance Regiment had spotted a powerful German armoured column moving out of the town of Vire; an AOP was required immediately in order to bring down a barrage onto that column. There was also a report of enemy activity in the area around La Herbelliere, where the 2nd Northamptonshire Yeomanry HQ was located, to the northeast of Vire. Alex immediately grabbed his message board yelling to the Eighth AGRA Duty Officer that he would fly the sortie.

Chapter 10

Homecoming!

Alex, and his observer Sergeant Bill Wright, dashed to their aircraft, TW348, which had been refuelled that morning and still had approximately ten imperial gallons of fuel available to them. They were ready for immediate action, pre-flight checked and with the '22 set' pre-tuned and 'netted' to work with Eighth AGRA from their previous mission. Alex and Bill were very quickly airborne and setting course for the town of Vire where the advance reconnaissance units had last been reported. Alex set the aircraft into a cruise climb at eighty miles per hour before levelling off at one thousand seven hundred and fifty feet above mean sea level, this altitude gave him sufficient height for terrain clearance whilst giving him, and Bill, a good all-round view of activities on the ground, and of any hostile threats from above.

As soon as Alex had levelled the Auster into the cruise at ninety miles per hour, and had trimmed it for stable flight, he attempted to establish radio contact with the Eleventh Armoured Divisional HQ, callsign 'ironside sunray;' he got no response other than the crackle of static. Repeated attempts obtained no better results; he asked Bill to attempt to re-net the '22 set' to the eighth AGRA since he was still well within the operational range of the set. Bill proved the set operational by re-tuning to their Squadron frequency and establishing clear communications with their Operations Officer. Further attempts were made to establish contact with units of the Eleventh Armoured Division but without success. Alex decided that he would continue with his recce and attempt to direct a shoot, if necessary, using his Operations Officer as a rear link communicating with the Gunners. Bill worked diligently making further attempts to contact the Gunners and finally managed to raise the Ayrshire Yeomanry a Field Regiment allocated as Divisional Artillery to the Eleventh Armoured Division.

As they breasted a ridge close to the village of Beaulieu they spotted Armoured Fighting Vehicles moving northwest towards the A177 highway not far from Vire. Almost immediately they came under fire from nearby enemy infantry which was moving up with the armour. A line of bullet holes was stitched across the right-hand side instrument panel, wrecking the 22 set, and through the right-side cockpit glazing. Alex felt several thumps in his left thigh, shoulder and back: he knew that he had been hit. His immediate reaction was lightning fast; he pulled the Auster round in a steep climbing turn to the right whilst ramming the throttle plunger fully forward to get full power from his engine which thankfully had not been hit. His manoeuvre took his aircraft away from the source of the ground fire that had caught them unawares, and it put the under-seat armour plating between him and the machine gun which was still shooting at him. He rolled out of the turn before the airspeed bled away towards seventy miles per hour at which speed the aircraft would enter an aerodynamic stall due to the increase in stalling speed as the bank angle was increased. He was starting to succumb to the shock of having been hit hard by several bullets, feeling lightheaded he relaxed the back pressure on the stick and retarded the throttle to a degree that seemed right for cruising power. He looked back to check on Bill, he saw him slumped in his seat with a line of bloody holes across his body. Alex's first thoughts were that he must get back to the guns to report the enemy positions, and to get Bill to the nearest Field Hospital: then recognising his own wounds he decided that he had better have the Medics take a look at him as well. He fumbled for the first aid kit and tried to staunch the flow of blood from his thigh but found that his left arm was almost useless, and he could not tie off the field dressing to bind the wound.

The Auster had settled into a gentle climb since the power setting that Alex had instinctively set was slightly above that needed for the normal ninety miles per hour cruising speed. The aircraft was in perfect trim to sustain this speed and in the virtually still air the wings remained level due to the natural stability that was design feature of the aircraft. Alex drifted in and out of consciousness as the little aircraft flew steadily northwards past his Advanced Landing Ground, then between Bayeaux and Caen before crossing the Channel coast over the Invasion Beaches. As the fuel was consumed the aircraft became lighter and continued to climb as the English Channel was crossed. A Radar Operator on the south coast of England spotted a return that was not showing an IFF, Identification Friend or Foe, blip and reported it to his Sector Operations Room Controller. A flight of Spitfires returning from a sortie over Normandy were vectored onto the target. The Leader quickly spotted the Auster as they approached the English coast near Selsey Bill. The Spitfire Flight swung in to attack the intruder from the rear, the Flight Leader saw the black and white invasion stripes on the Auster and slowing his fighter he saw that there was a two-man crew, neither of whom were responded to the presence of his Flight as they came up alongside and overtook them. The Spitfires had to slow to a speed close to that which they used for their approach to landing: they took up defensive positions around the little Auster to escort it to a nearby airfield. The Pilot of the Auster remained unresponsive as the Spitfire Leader attempted to direct him towards Tangmere, and then to Goodwood. Alex was drifting in and out of consciousness. When conscious he was vaguely aware that he was flying but he could not make out any details of his surroundings, everything was hazy, and he felt that he was looking down a foggy tunnel. Eventually, the Spitfire Pilot spotted the steel plank strip which formed the south to north runway at Upham Manor dead on the nose. The Auster's propellor seemed to be slowing and the nose of the aircraft dropped toward the runway. The Auster's fuel was exhausted, and the engine was dying. The Auster's nose nodded down and up a couple of times before a stable nose down attitude was established. Eventually approximately a quarter of a mile short of the runway the engine stopped completely with the propellor windmilling in airflow. Alex was roused into a semiconscious state as the engine quit. The now gliding Auster cleared the boundary hedge and once in the ground effect the nose rose, Alex's subconscious reflex on sensing his closeness to the ground had been to pull the control stick back to bring the aircraft to a level attitude as it settled onto the runway. It bounced before settling again and rolling to stop before it ran off the steel planks onto the grass. Alex was again unconscious.

The Emergency Ground Crews had been alerted to the incoming aircraft following a telephone call from the RAF Sector Station at Tangmere. The Flight of Spitfires swept through the overhead before circling to both provide cover and to see what happened once the

Auster had landed. The Crash Tender screeched to a halt beside the Auster. The Rescue Crew jumped out to deal with any possible fire and to lift the two men, who remained motionless in their seats, from the cockpit. Alex was carefully extracted from his seat and placed on the ground beside the port mainwheel of his aircraft. His eyes fluttered open and he spoke in a whisper, "tell Jane I'll be bit late for dinner." With a tickle of blood forming at the corner of mouth his eyes glazed over and the last of his breath left his body with a soft sigh.

The Rescue Crew had a difficult task extricating Bill's dead body from the Observer's seat on the righthand side at the rear of the cockpit. The bodies of the two men were covered over before being loaded into an ambulance to be taken to the Airbase's Medical Centre. The identity of the Pilot was quickly established from his 'dog' tags, and some of the Ground Crew recognised him as having been a Flight Commander attached to the USAAF at RAF Upham Manor prior to his departure to join his AOP Squadron only months before his unexpected arrival in his shot-up Auster. The buzz of conversation round the Airbase was focussed on the untimely and surprising return of Captain Shooter to his former Airbase. The RAF and the British Army were notified that one of their aircraft had turned up unannounced, damaged by gunfire, at RAF Upham Manor. Also, the two crew members, Captain Alexander James Shooter and Sergeant William Wright both of the Royal Artillery, had died of their wounds. The Royal Artillery was quick to reclaim their own, and to arrange for the funerals of both men who were to be laid to rest with full military honours.

Chapter 11

Laid to rest

The American technical team took charge of the aircraft, dragging it away to the maintenance hangar to await its eventual return to the RAF. Weeks passed and the RAF showed no sign of wanting to recover the airplane anytime soon, so Master Sergeant Joe Kennedy decided that it would be better to prepare it for transport by road. He removed the wings, and the propellor, before moving it to the back of the hanger where it would be both safe from further damage and out of the way of his teams of airframe and engine mechanics. As more time went by Joe decided that if he didn't act soon the engine would start to suffer from internal corrosion. He removed the engine from the airframe; a quick inspection showed the engine to be in pristine condition, pretty much as the day it had come out the factory back in the States. He cleaned it up, drained out the oil and refilled it with passivating fluid, before he packed it in a storage crate which he placed beside the airframe at the back of the hanger. The time came for the USAAF to pack up and depart from RAF Upham Manor: Joe was busy disposing of everything that the Air Force didn't want to take with them. He had his mechanics complete the crating up of Captain Alex's dismantled Auster, USAAF was stencilled on the crates. The aircraft seemed to have been abandoned by the RAF and since it wasn't on any USAAF inventories Joe left it where it was waiting for the RAF to recover when they were ready so to do. The Chamberlain family, who had owned the land before it was converted to an airfield, had permission to cut the grass and take hay crops off the field. After the departure of the USAAF the Chamberlains were given permission to use the now almost empty maintenance hangar to store the hay cut from the field. The crop for nineteen forty-eight was stored as usual in the almost empty hanger. The stack completely obscured the crates which were positioned along the rear wall. The farmer continued using the stored hay for his livestock feed and as the years passed the haystack was replenished and worked down several times over, the crated aircraft was buried.

On Tuesday the fifteenth of August nineteen forty-four, Captain Alexander James Shooter MC was to be laid to rest with full military honours, at St Andrews churchyard in his and Jane's adopted home village of Middle Down. The Guard of Honour was unusual in that it was to be made up of both British and American troops. The day dawned with a clear sky and wispy banks of mist swirling around the hedgerows in a light breeze. As the sun rose higher and its power to warm the earth grew the mists lifted and finally dispersed, as Alex's coffin arrived from RAF Upham Manor on a Gun Carriage. It was drawn by an American Army Air Force Jeep, it was driven by Master Sergeant Joe Kennedy. The Guard of Honour drawn from Alex's Regiment, D Flight, and a USAAF Contingent from RAF Upham Manor lined the roadway leading up to the Church. A small party of family mourners lead by Jane Shooter, together with both Alex's and her parents, followed the bearer party carrying the Union Flag draped Coffin. His number one dress service cap, gloves, and his sword had been placed on top of the Coffin. As the procession entered the Medieval Church for the Funeral Service prior to the Interment the Village Organist was playing the 'Dead March' from Handel's Oratorio 'Saul.' The Service was conducted by Squadron Leader Godfrey, the Chaplain at RAF Old Sarum, with the Vicar of the Parish of St Andrews in attendance. The Order of Service was relatively short; the Vicar welcomed the mourners to St Andrews whilst expressing his condolences to the family of the deceased and invited Squadron Leader Godfrey to conduct the Service. Squadron Leader Godfrey lead the congregation in prayer before they sang the hymn "Abide with me." One of the Honour Guard from D Flight read Psalm 121. Captain William Ollie Squires, who was in Italy with 654 Squadron, had asked that his father Lt. Colonel Frederick Squires DSO would read the Eulogy on his behalf. Lt Colonel Squires read the lines penned by his son, his normally stiff upper lip quivered with emotion. Ollie had written of his recollections of their school days, and training as RA Officers. He detailed their close friendship and some of their many escapades together. He closed with moving valediction to his fallen friend and brother-in-law. Prayers for the Deceased, followed by the Lord's Prayer, preceded the Commendation and Farewell.

The Congregation withdrew to the strains of Handel's choral music 'See the conquering hero comes.' The Burial Party was ready at the graveside for the Committal which was conducted by Squadron Leader Godfrey. As the then bare Coffin was solemnly lowered into the ground an Honour Party consisting of three USAAF and three RA Gunners under the command of the Station Warrant Officer at RAF Old Sarum fired three volleys over the grave. The Mourners sadly paid their last respects and each dropped a handful of soil onto the coffin as they moved away from the graveside.

The family and a small group of friends, who had attended the Funeral, gathered for refreshments and A Wake in the cottage that Alex and Jane had bought in Middle Down shortly after his posting to RAF Upham Manor. It was a subdued affair in which reminiscences of good times, and bad, were shared between the guests and a final toast to the departed had been drunk.

Jane, suddenly overcome by her tiredness and her sense of loss excused herself from Alex's parents, both of whom were staying the night with her, and took herself to her bedroom. Memories of her time with Alex tumbled through her mind: from the earliest when Ollie had introduced his best friend to her whilst they were teenagers, to the happy days at Cambridge during his time at 22 EFTS, and then their time snatched with short passes out from duty, and longer weekend passes. Then there was their whirlwind engagement and quiet marriage in Thrapston followed by their few honeymoon days in Bournemouth on the south coast. Even though the beach was mined and wired as part of the anti-invasion defences the Promenade and the cliff top walks were open, here they had enjoyed their evenings walking and sitting looking out over the English Channel engrossed in their love for each other and thinking of a future together. She particularly treasured the period of leave that they had enjoyed immediately prior to Alex re-joining D Flight and then his assignment to active service with 659 Squadron at RAF East Grinstead in Surrey.

Their last day together had been on Sunday the fourteenth of May. There were bitter-sweet memories; they had enjoyed their bonding intimacy during a long lie in that morning. Jane recalled the sense of oneness they shared that morning and the feeling of being removed from all the cares of the world outside the bubble of their being. The day had been spent idly in the garden even though the skies were cloudy, and the temperature was rather cool for the time of year. All too soon, whilst preparing their lunch rations, Jane realised that their idyll was coming to a close and that Alex had to get his kit together and load up their little Austin Seven car in readiness for his drive along the coast to his new Squadron. The journey would take him at least three hours and he wanted to be on his way by four o'clock at the very latest. He had contacted the Mess Steward at RAF East Grinstead to "warn in" giving his estimated time of arrival as seven o'clock in the evening, hopefully in time for dinner and ensuring that his room would be ready for him on arrival. As Jane lay on her bed that evening, she comforted herself knowing that she had part of her beloved with her: she knew for certain that she was three months pregnant and that their child would be born in mid-February.

In an attempt to manage her grief at the loss of her beloved Alex she threw herself into her duties as a Section Officer in the FANY. A few months later her Commanding Officer called her into her office to inform her that as an expectant mother she would have to stand down from all her duties at the end of the second week in November. Valentine Shooter was delivered on his due date the fourteenth of February, Saint Valentine's Day, as a healthy seven-pound eight-ounce baby boy. According to his paternal grandmother he was the spitting image of his father.

Part 3

West Sussex August 1967 ~August 1969 and Normandy August 1969.

Chapter 12

It's here!

Valentine, Jasper, Giles, and Charlie talked long into the afternoon about the history of RAF Upham Manor and the characters who had made the Old White Hart inn their home from home during the latter years of World War Two. Upon hearing the story of his father's miraculous return to RAF Upham Manor and his dying words Valentine felt a surge of love for his father and was again moved to tears. It took quite a while for him to compose himself sufficiently to speak. When he did regain the power of speech, he said I'm starting to understand why I was drawn to the aerodrome this morning.

Giles glanced over in his Jasper's direction and softly said "it's been almost twenty-five years since. I think the lad has been called to resurrect her." "Perhaps so" responded Jasper who turned to Valentine and putting his arm over the younger man's shoulders said, "there's a bit more of the story that we haven't told you yet and it pertains to why you came to us, and why you were urged to 'find it.' Valentine looked up at Jasper with a slightly puzzled expression "go on?" he queried. "Well," replied Jasper, "as you now know Joe was a mechanical genius and quite a squirrel where it came to collecting and storing anything that was repairable. When your dad's aeroplane was dragged into the hangar it looked decidedly worse for wear, the Americans didn't want it and although the RAF knew about it nobody took any notice and eventually it was pushed right into a corner at the back of the hangar. Joe decided after a month or two that the engine had to be taken care of to protect against internal corrosion. He drained the sump, flushed the oil system, and filled it with passivating fluid. He also derigged the airframe so that it wouldn't take up so much space, the wings and tail were riddled with bullet holes as was the fuselage. He remarked that it was very strange and lucky for your dad that none of the flying controls, the fuel tank, or the engine were damaged. He put the wings into a set of wing boxes, greased all the bearings and pulleys and wrapped the engine in oiled cloth. The wooden propellor was taken off, cleaned, and covered with wax before being tightly wrapped in oiled brown paper and boxed up. The boxed wings were leaned up against the back wall. Similarly, the fuselage was crated along with the lift struts, tailplanes, elevators, tail fin and rudder. The undercarriage legs were placed within the cockpit before the fuselage crate was nailed up and placed against the wing boxes so as to prevent them from being accidentally knocked down. The boxes of parts that had been removed were stacked on the fuselage crate and behind the tail end of the crate. The whole lot took up no more than five feet by forty-five feet of floor space. As the war progressed the American training was wound down and the Base became a Maintenance Unit before it was finally handed back to the RAF. As I said before that was when Joe "sold" me the Jeep, they took everything they needed and departed. We had a right royal party in the Old White Hart with the Rear Echelon Party on their last night with us. What was left behind technically became property of the RAF. Squadron Leader Cross had been posted to Tangmere effective from the day the USAAF formally vacated the aerodrome, and several weeks later a young Flying Officer, who was recovering from wounds that he had collected whilst flying a Hawker Typhoon fighter-bomber over Normandy, was posted as the RAF Liaison Officer in his place. I can't for the life of me recall his name and he was invalided out of the service shortly after VE-Day. Once the Americans had gone the station was placed on a care and maintenance basis with a small cadre of pencil pushers and airmen to keep the place neat and tidy. The Station was by then under the Command of the Group Captain based at Tangmere, Archie Cross came over from time to time to see that all was as it should be and we carried on taking the hay crop off the field. The hangar in which your dad's aircraft was still stored was made available to us to store the cut hay and for us to park our machinery. Archie must have forgotten about the aeroplane in the crates at the back of the hangar. It wasn't too long before the War Office made it known that they were to close the station for good and that we could have it back if we wanted it for the price that they had paid upon requisitioning the land. They returned the Property Deeds to us and included a statement to the effect that all the buildings and their contents were to be included in the Transfer of Ownership."

Valentine, wide eyed excitedly questioned "are you telling me that my father's aeroplane is in that hangar right now?" Jasper and Giles wreathed in smiles both nodded their agreement. "Yes lad," Giles said "and what's more I believe that your dad was telling you to go and find it. What we need to do now is to take you back to the field and see what we can find behind the hay stacked in that hangar." Valentine was on his feet in a flash and was heading towards the door when Jasper called him back. "Hold on, she's been waiting there these twenty odd years a few more minutes won't matter; but you left your mother's house this morning before she was out of her bed and she has no idea where are or what you are doing. I think that it would be a good idea to contact her to let her know that you are alright and give her an idea of when you might be back. Don't you?" Charlie took Valentine by the elbow and steered him through the Public Bar and into the kitchen; he pointed to the telephone on side table beside which was an old, but comfortable, wheel back chair. "There's the 'phone, give her a call and take all the time you need, there's no charge".

Twenty minutes later Valentine re-joined his newfound friends in the snug. "Mum said that she is coming straight over, she wants to meet you all and wants to be there when we pull dad's 'plane out." Giles laughed loudly at that, "there's damn great pile of hay in that hangar and whilst we can wriggle ourselves over it to get to the machine, we will have to move a ton or two of the stuff before we can start to get the old girl out. There's also a few bits of machinery in the way." He paused, "I know you are dead keen young Valentine, but we will have to make some time to get that little job done." Giles continued after a minute or two, "you are an Aeronautical Engineer, aren't you? And, you have a Private Pilot's Licence. So, if she is restorable why don't we start making some plans to do just that? After all its less than two years to the Twenty-fifth Anniversary of the 'D-Day' landings in Normandy and I know that there is going to be a big celebration over there to commemorate it. You could fly over to Caen and participate in the festivities." As he contemplated the event a sad expression crept over his face. "I'll be going with my old mates from the REME and the Eleventh Armoured Division. I was with them through the campaign in Normandy and then on through Holland and into Northwest Germany." He paused "I was one of the lucky ones, I came home in one piece, and to have a home to come back to." He paused, "in some ways it will be hard to go back there, but I have good mates who never left, and I must go and visit them." Charlie got up and fetched another round of beers, whilst the others sat quietly, each with his own thoughts and memories. Giles lifted his glass and called a toast "absent friends" he said, the others joined in. After he had taken a good pull at his beer Giles started to reminisce about his military service and the days of his youth before he had volunteered to join the Royal Engineers as a Mechanic.

"I was rather like dad's mate Joe Kennedy" he said. "I learned as a youngster to work with, and on, the farm machinery. Mind you we were working with horses then, but we had a mechanical hay cutter and a 'McCormick' reaper-binder for the wheat and barley harvest. Just before war broke out in nineteen thirty-nine dad bought a Fordson tractor to speed up the work of ploughing and seeding the crops. It was a right 'basket' to start. She had two fuel tanks, one for paraffin the other for petrol. She had to be primed with petrol and hand cranked until she fired, and then kept on the petrol once she started and warmed up. Then you had to switch over to paraffin to put her to work. She could be a bitch to start. She kicked back at me a few times taking the crank handle out of my hands and darned near caught my wrists as it flew round the wrong way. Anyway, I had done well at Chichester High School for boys and was awarded my Matriculation Certificate. I was good at sciences and mathematics so I decided that I would try for a place at university to read engineering. However, at that time the Prime Minister, Neville Chamberlain, had come back from Germany waving his 'bit of paper' declaring 'peace in our time.' I was not one bit convinced by that declaration so as well as making applications to several universities for a place, I also applied to join the Corps of Royal Engineers, in the Territorial Army as a Private. Because I had tinkered with the Fordson tractor and I had an old Douglas K32 motorcycle, which wasn't the most reliable of machines, I had a fair working knowledge of engines, transmissions, and rudimentary lighting systems. Dad had a brand-new Vauxhall 10, but I wasn't allowed to touch that." Jasper grinned and said, "you were mad enough with that Douglas, I wasn't going to let you tear about in my pride and joy!" "Anyway," continued Giles, "to cut a long story short, I started training with a Royal Engineers detachment based at Littlehampton. After seven or eight months I was called into the CO's office, I was a bit apprehensive but couldn't think that I had done anything wrong! The CO didn't beat about the bush 'Chamberlain,' he said, 'you have good skills and get on well with your fellows. I'm promoting you to Lance-corporal with immediate effect. What do you say to that?' I was stunned, all I could say was 'thank you Sir.' He took a pair of chevrons from his desk draw, handed them to me and said, 'get them sewn up immediately, dismiss.' I was as pleased as Punch. "

Mid-summer nineteen thirty-nine we were at our annual training camp near Stockbridge, we were working with a regular Engineer Squadron, and Yeomanry Armoured Regiments who were also on their annual camp training fortnight, one of which I was to serve alongside later in the war. They were a great bunch of lads, the Northamptonshire Yeomanry, they had very few armoured vehicles at that time and had arrived at the camp in a mixed bag of civilian vehicles and a couple of lorries. They exercised with some old Mark V tanks left on charge from the Great War and a few Vickers light tanks on loan from a regular Royal Armoured Corps unit. Whilst we were there I was approached by the Major in charge of a regular RE Squadron. He asked me if I had considered joining the Regular

Army. He had seen me at work and had reports of my conduct. I hadn't given it a thought until then. On our last day at Stockbridge, I asked permission to see the Major and told him that I had thought about joining the Regulars in the Engineers. He said, 'good man, I had a feeling that you would. You are aware that you would have to drop back to a Private, but I'm sure that will be for a short period only. Let's get the paperwork going, shall we?' So it was that I found myself in the Regular Army just before Hitler kicked off by invading Poland and we were suddenly at war.

My Squadron was sent to St Nazaire with the British Expeditionary Force to come under the Command of the First Corps on the Franco-Belgian border. My mechanical skills were well known, and I was promoted to Lance-corporal again working on the maintenance of our troop vehicles and heavy equipment. We spent months during the phoney war being moved from pillar to post up and down the line wondering when, and where, the Germans would attack. On the occasions we were posted to locations behind the Maginot line we felt safe, and we let our hair down. Rude, and licentious, soldiery we were at that time. We got the shock of our lives when the Jerries broke through the Line taking Fort Eban Emael in a coup-de-main operation by glider borne troops. They poured through the Ardennes and we were suddenly fighting for our lives as the blitzkrieg hit us. It was a mad scramble to try and hold a line whilst others were retreating towards the coast. Our lads were left mining bridges, and then getting the hell out of it to the next line of defence. What a shambles it was, communications were breaking down, refugees clogging the roads, half the time we didn't know where our Squadron HQ was. Eventually, I got to the port in Dunkirk and was taken off the Mole onto a Destroyer, and home safely. I came back here for a period of convalescent leave, walking wounded I was, before going off to East Anglia with the Squadron to work on coastal defences." Jasper chipped in as Giles took a minute to draw on his ale. "What he didn't mention was that he came home as an acting Lance- sergeant with a recommendation for the award of a Military Medal in recognition of his heroics on the Albert Canal, where he copped a few shell splinters in his backside." "Enough of that dad" huffed Giles "I was just doing my job; the Army was grateful for my service; blood, toil, tears and sweat at that time."

Giles continued his reminiscences: "By nineteen forty-three I was promoted to full Sergeant and with the reorganisation of the Army the Corps of the Royal Electrical and Mechanical Engineers was formed. The Armoured Divisions had been responsible for their own maintenance, rescue, and recovery of their vehicles but it had been shown to be inefficient. The tank crews were trained as Driver-Mechanics and Radio operator-Mechanics but they were better deployed in action rather than at a rear echelon repairing their vehicles and communications gear. As a Mechanic I was transferred to the new Corps as soon as it was formed. We were sent all over the country on training courses with the manufacturers of tanks, armoured cars, carriers, Quad gun tractors and guns, not to mention lorries and transporters. On April first, All Fool's Day, nineteen forty-four I was posted to Driffield in Yorkshire to work-up with the Eleventh Armoured Division where I met my old friends of the Second Northants Yeomanry who by then were the Divisional Armoured Reconnaissance Regiment. Almost immediately we were on the move south to the Aldershot area in preparation of the invasion of Europe."

He stopped speaking, his eyes in a seeming thousand-yard stare for several seconds, before he picked up his tankard and slowly took another deep draft of ale. Still with that faraway look he started his tale again: "We landed in Normandy on the eleventh of July, through the Mulberry harbour at Arromanches, my Squadron was landed with B Squadron of the Yeomanry: they had been held back in England as the Divisional Reserve. I was then a Squadron Sergeant Major so didn't get up to the front line very often, we had a backlog of recovered Cromwell tanks which had been damaged during Operation Epsom. We also had some Sherman tanks that had belonged to other Regiments in the Eleventh Armoured which were brought back to our base near Bayeaux. They were needed to be back into action as quickly as we could manage the task, or we had to cannibalise them to keep others going. Also, we had to keep the echelon supply vehicles up to the mark. Thankfully, the 'Recce Troop' and elements of B Squadron had insisted that they would not use the American 'Honey' or as we called it the 'Stuart' light tank and had equipped with the more manoeuvrable, and more easily hidden, Universal Carriers and Humber scout cars in their place.

The Rear Echelon lads were the real unsung heroes of the army. They kept the fighting troops supplied with everything they needed to stay in action. A typical lorry load would have cans of fuel, engine oil, armour piercing and high explosive shells for the tanks' main guns, these included six-pounders on some of the Cromwells, Seventy- fives on others and a few with Ninety-five millimetre howitzers, all had BESA machine guns that needed belts pre-loaded with point three-inch rimless ammunition that was the same as the 7.92 millimetre Mauser rounds used by the Jerries. Again, Giles paused momentarily lost in thought. Finally, he said "sorry I digress; too many memories."

After another swig of ale from his now almost empty tankard, he resumed his narrative. "Following Operation Goodwood there were a great many vehicles to bring in. Most of the Shermans had 'brewed up and burned out' when hit by anti-tank shells, the Jerries called the Shermans 'Tommy Cookers' our lads sarcastically called them 'Ronsons' after the cigarette lighter which had the sales line 'lights first-time every-time.' Some of them had to be hosed out before we could start to work on them! We had to work with the Forward Delivery Squadrons to ensure the replacement vehicles were ready for action in all respects. Then we were plunged into Operation Bluecoat running alongside the Yanks who were pushing south through Saint Lo towards Avranches, along the course of the Drome River, on Operation Cobra. General Roberts' lads of the Eleventh Armoured did a fantastic job, running and guarding the American left flank and getting way ahead of them down to Vire. They were as mad as hell when they were told to pull back and leave Vire to the Yanks. I remember talking to one of the Troop Corporals from B Squadron who I had first become friends with at that first pre-war camp at Stockbridge, he was called Jack. I can't recall his second name, he was a Tank Commander, Driver-Mechanic, who had been seconded to the Royal Armoured Corps school at Bovingdon for a couple of years before being returned to the Yeomanry in the Spring of forty-four in readiness for the Invasion. He had pushed on with his recce to the outskirts of the town when the Mayor and a few other people approached his Cromwell tank. The Mayor passed up bottle of wine for the crew and told Jack that there were no Germans in the town, and it was theirs for the taking. He was more than surprised after reporting his position to be ordered to pull back to La Bistierre, where he would find the Regimental HQ, for further orders. They didn't know, but the top brass did, that Hitler had ordered his Panzers to start an operation which was designed to punch through the Allied lines and stop the Americans from reaching Avranches. The Eleventh

Armoured were pulled back to shield the Yanks and stop the Jerry punch through their left flank. That was a messy action. I was sent off from our base at Bayeaux to our forward position at Le Beny Bocage. From there I set off with a full crew in a turretless Churchill recovery vehicle to bring in, or repair if we could, elements of the Second Northants HQ Squadron that had been attacked in an orchard near La Herbellierre. That morning, like others over several days before, had started with a thickish mist that took time to lift and be burned off by the sun which then gave us some really lovely clear days. We had started off from our Forward Echelon position as the mist was beginning to lift and navigation hadn't been easy to begin with. Thinking back, I recall that it was in the early afternoon when we were on a main road between the villages of Le Reculey and Beaulieu that I ordered my Driver to turn off into a green lane, the Bocage, that was lined with earthen banks and high hedges. As we entered the Bocage, I saw an AOP Auster heading in a southerly direction at a low altitude. There must have been a Jerry unit not too far from Beaulieu because the next thing I knew was the Auster in a steep turn to the right towards us and then, instead of diving for the cover provided by the lie of land, it climbed away towards the north.

Having been alerted to the enemy forces to my front I lost sight of the aircraft as I looked around for any immediate threat to us and I ordered my Driver to halt whilst we called Eleventh Armoured HQ with the intelligence we had gathered, and to request further orders. I was redirected to find, and stay with, elements of 'B' Squadron of the Yeomanry who were believed to be in fields near the main road at La Bistierre, between Le Beny Bocage and Vire, not far from Beaulieu. We found them and joined in with the defence of their Laager: all of us dismounted and ended up fighting, at close quarters, on foot in hedgerows in the dark and thickening mist. My crew and I had "Sten" guns, Webley pistols and a few 'Mills bombs.' That was nasty work that night we took a few casualties, thankfully not too many. We cleaned up as much as we could in the morning and went off to find the damaged HQ Squadron tank and the Adjutant's wrecked halftrack in an orchard at La Herbalierre the following day."

At this point Valentine's vivacious mother came into the Inn looking for the group. Valentine spotted her as she made her somewhat hurried entrance, all heads in the group turned at his exclamation "Mother!" At first, she remonstrated with her son for going out without leaving a note telling her where he had gone. Then she relented and hugged him before asking to be introduced to his companions. She eventually recognised Charlie when he offered his hand for her to shake. "Well fancy that you are still here after all these years and I've been living not far away in Middle Down. Mind after Alex died, I couldn't bring myself to come here." Charlie beamed at her, "you were a young slip of a gel when you came down here on leave to be with Alex, you hadn't been long married as I recall." "Yes," she replied, "we were married from my home in East Northamptonshire just before Alex was posted here, I was serving in the 'Fanys' at the time and had just wangled a posting to be near him. Valentine looked shocked at his mother's utterance, "Fanys?" I thought you drove an ambulance and were a Nurse?" "I did, silly" she laughingly shot back "First Aid Nursing Yeomanry although we weren't really qualified Nurses, and we didn't just drive ambulances. We were also Motor–mechanics and drove whatever was required of us. Then turning to the others, she said "as you know I am Alex's widow and Valentine's mother, he was born on Saint Valentine's Day nineteen forty-five, almost seven months after Alex was killed in action, hence his name."

Charlie spoke up, "I can't quite recall your name, Joan? Jean? No Jane, that's it, Jane, isn't it?" "Well remembered Charlie" replied Jane, "you really have a good memory for names and faces" "Ah, I never forget a pretty face m' gel; especially one as good looking as you and being married to Alex. I can't recall how many times he showed me your photo'!" Their small talk, reminiscences and plans for the following day took them into the early evening before Jane stood up and declared that she and Valentine had to get home or the stew that she had simmering on the kitchen range would be as dry as a bone. They agreed to meet again in the Old White Hart the following lunchtime and to continue their reunion. The Chamberlains had a busy farm to run and Alex had his own important arrangements to make regarding his future before they could meet again.

Chapter 13

Recovery

The following morning Valentine called his Mentor at Cranfield to let him know that he had decided to follow an academic career and that he would like to enrol in the faculty to undertake a Doctorate in Aeronautical Engineering if that was possible. His mentor snapped him up immediately, telling him to be back at Cranfield at the start of the second week in September to complete his enrolment. He also asked what Valentine wished to work on. "Battle damage to airframes, aircraft systems and methods to mitigate the effects thereof" was the immediate response.

At lunchtime Jane and Valentine set off in Jane's old, but beautifully maintained, Sunbeam Talbot Sports Tourer to meet up with Jasper and Giles at the Old White Hart. Jasper's Jeep was parked under the Smoke Room windows as before, beside it was a mud-spattered Mark 1 Land Rover. Jane drove further up the yard to park her car and they entered the inn through a door that led into a short passageway with an open door giving onto the Public Bar straight ahead of them and a recessed door to their right giving access to the Smoke Room. They found Jasper and Giles in the Bar with pint tankards in hand. There was also a pile of ham and cheese sandwiches on an enormous serving platter on the table between them, a pot of homemade apple chutney stood beside the platter. "Come on, tuck in, we can't eat all of these ourselves or we will be fatter than our porkers" said Giles cheerily. Jasper promptly called for a pint of 'home brewed' in a glass tankard and asked Jane what she would take. "A half of Indian Pale if you please Jasper" she replied. Drinks duly served and tasted; the pile of sandwiches was attacked with gusto. Sandwich in one hand and tankard in the other Giles informed them that the lads had started on moving the stored agricultural equipment and would then be starting on the hay in the hangar. He reckoned that they should be able to reach the dismantled Auster early in the afternoon, although it would be late before there would be enough room to manoeuvre the airframe, wings, and boxes of parts out to the front part of the hangar for inspection.

At two o'clock Charlie called "time" as he collected the empty glasses and headed for the cellar. The other patrons drifted out to return to their work, travels, or in the case of the older men their gardens and allotments. Jasper, Giles, Valentine, and Jane hung back discussing possible plans of action once the aircraft was exhumed from its tomb. All were agreed that if it was humanly possible the aircraft must be restored. If possible, it had to participate in the Twenty-fifth Anniversary celebrations marking the D-Day landings and the ensuing battle for Normandy which were being planned.

Giles, ever practical, remarked that getting spares and parts wouldn't be easy and that it could prove expensive. Valentine shook his head. "Not as difficult as you may think Giles. We have Auster Aiglet trainers at Cranfield, and we have no difficulty keeping them maintained. Spares and consumables aren't hard to come by. British Executive and General Aviation Limited has the production details of all the Auster marques and they provide a full product support service. Also, there is a Pilot's Club we can go to for help and advice. Several of their members have successfully completed restorations and rebuilds and have gained full Certificates of Airworthiness from the Board of Trade's Air Registration Board." Jane interrupted rather impatiently, "stop talking about it and let's get over to the airfield and see just what has got to be done." Calling "goodbye" to Charlie they made for their cars, Jane and Valentine were the first away and set off at the usual sporty pace that Jane was accustomed to maintain. They arrived on the hangar apron a good five minutes before first Giles, in the Land Rover, and then Jasper, in his Jeep, arrived.

The apron was quite crowded with the old farm machinery which had been hauled out from the one-time hangar using the ancient Fordson Major tractor which had worked the farm since Jasper's father had bought it new before the War. Jane remarked to Giles with a girlish laugh, "looks like you're preparing for an antiques auction with that old stuff." A sizable pile of hay was growing to one side of the open doors as Jasper's farm hands worked to remove the enormous amount that was stored towards the back of the shed.

They were greeted by one of the older farm hands, Billy Brewster's much creased and weather-beaten face lit up in recognition of his visitors. He showed a gap-toothed grin as he greeted Valentine and Jane, "Ah, yer must be young Adrian," and turning to Jane he continued "and yer gotta be missus Shooter." Valentine and Jane both laughed before Valentine managed to say, that's a fine compliment to my dad Alexander but I'm Valentine Shooter. Val to my friends and this is my mum, Jane. What shall we call you?" "Yer the spitting image, the double, of yer dad and I just called you Adrian. Sorry I should have recalled better and knowed he was Alex, because I saw yer as him like he was when he were here. Ahr yes; me, I'm Ol' Bill to everyone. That lanky feller, over by the old reaper binder, he's called 'Gnasher'; his real name is Ted Nash and the young lad a' top the hay bales he's 'Jockey' cos he's a small lad and rides 'osses like he were born to it; his proper name is Charlie Naylor. They're both smashing blokes, hearts of gold they 'ave. Yer can trust 'em with yer life." "Well Bill, I reckon that we will be friends, and long may that be the case" said Jane with a beautiful wide smile.

"Anyhow" said Bill, "we must be getting on moving all this hay so as we can get to Captain Shooter's airyplane before the pubs are open again. "With that he stomped away on his bowed legs; his back bent showing his age and the toll of years of backbreaking labour on the farm. "Can we help?" asked Jane. "Best you stand back 'til we get a bit of order going on 'ere" replied Bill, calling back over his shoulder. "Can't have you getting hurt in this mess, can we." "Quite right Bill" called Giles as he clambered out of his Land Rover. "You two stand back for a bit, there will be plenty for you to get stuck into once we've cleared a way through to storage boxes and the aircraft itself."

After a few minutes Valentine and Jane wandered away to look at the other airfield buildings. Valentine had a brainwave; he ran back to Giles and Jasper who were connecting a three-share plough to the hydraulic hitch on Jasper's almost brand-new David Brown tractor. Valentine called to them "what's in the sheds over by the old Watch Office? Could we start to clear one of them for use as a store and workshop for the smaller items that will need to be renovated, or rebuilt, or restored? Is that something mum and I could be getting on with right now to make ourselves useful?"

"Good thinking lad" replied Jasper, "hold on a minute while I finish here, and we'll take a look at which would be best for the job." He paused, thinking for a while before saying "we're going to put this machinery in the old MT garage. There's the MT office and the old workshop that runs down the side of the building. There's nothing in them that is of any use or value so you could make a start in there. We'll bring the two-wheel trailer round for you to chuck the rubbish into. Then we can cart it off, to burn or bury it out of harm's way. We can open out one of the aircraft dispersal sites."

Jane took one look into the old MT Section's offices and workshops which were garlanded with spiders' webs and covered in the dust of ages. She immediately declared that she was going home to get into some old clothes that would be more suitable for the tasks that lay ahead. She also said that she would bring brushes, buckets, mops, and cleaning materials so that the place could be made fit for human occupation. Valentine swiped away cobwebs and worked his way through the rooms making a closer inspection of the interior, and the stuff that had been left behind when the last occupants had shut them up in readiness for the decommissioning of the Station. There were old rusty tins, cans, and bottles; the labels of which were faded and not always readable. A couple of adjustable bench lamps with rusted shades were attached to the backs of the benches. There were also some sorry looking abandoned metal-working machines, filthy with grease and oil that had semi-solidified with age, dust, and other 'muck.' Valentine called back to Jasper, who had remained in the main garage area to organise the placement of the farm machinery that Giles was soon to bring in. "There are some machines in here that we might be able to overhaul and put to good use. There's a pillar drill, a small lathe, grinding wheels, a press, and a sheet metal roller which look as though they aren't quite ready to be scrapped just yet!

There was still a mountain of the animal foodstuff to remove before they would be able to reach the rear wall of the old hangar. Valentine shook off his jacket, grabbed a pitchfork, and set to work with the farm hands on the task before them whilst Giles and one of the farm hands set to making the pile on the apron into a neater, and safer stack. Before long they had removed enough hay for Valentine to scramble over the top and, with the aid of a torch, see the rear wall of the hanger and a stack of wooden crates of various sizes. Two large crates, approximately twenty by five by two feet in dimension were leaning against the rear wall behind another large crate, which resembled a large coffin some twenty feet long, six and a half feet wide and four feet deep that was partially buried under loose hay. A smaller crate some three by three by three feet was stacked on the broader end of the 'coffin.' A long, narrow and relatively shallow, box about six and half feet long by one foot wide and eight inches deep was stacked on the centre section of the 'coffin' on top of which stood a small cubic box approximately one foot four inches in size. There were faint paint marks on all the boxes indicating that they were once the property of the USAAF.

Valentine was overcome with a flood of emotions; it seemed that he was overjoyed and wrung out with sadness all in the same moment. *"I've found her dad, we've got her."* His thoughts were addressed to both him and to his father, whose presence he had been sensing increasingly keenly since he had first come across the old airfield buildings on the previous morning. With tears in his eyes, and with a choking voice, he called down to the rest of the team "there are large crates down behind the stack, we've found her." With that he redoubled his efforts to reduce the height of the stack of hay beneath his feet as others threw it out to Giles and those making the new stack on the apron. After about an hour they had created a valley through the haystack inside the hangar then they were then able to make their way through to the crates.

Even the smallest was quite heavy, but between them they manhandled it out into the sunshine. Like the others it was marked USAAF and had 'this way up' arrows marked on its sides. Jasper produced a pry-bar and a claw hammer from his Jeep's toolbox and soon he had the crate open. A layer of screwed up waxed brown paper was removed to reveal two roughly circular packages, again wrapped in waxed paper, each was supported vertically in the box on a one-inch diameter wooden dowel which itself was supported on side frames positioned halfway up the box. These were lifted out, the dowel removed, and unwrapped. "Main wheels I should think" said Giles as the final wrapping, this time of hessian sackcloth, was completely unwrapped. The wheels, still with the tyres in place looked as good as the day they were crated up: they even had traces of muck from the landing ground in Normandy on the walls and in the treads. Jasper looked on approvingly, "typical of Joe" he said, "always made a proper job of everything he touched." After a few seconds he added "it's almost as though he knew that this aeroplane was somehow special, and he made sure it was preserved for as long as it took."

Jane, who had been back on site for quite some time and had been cleaning out the office spaces in the former MT shed, announced that she really must take some photographs for the record and called the team together to stand around the opened box and its contents. "That should do for now." She then added "we must make an album of pictures as we get it all out into the open to send to your friend Joe" she said addressing Jasper. "You know lass, he'll be tickled pink to receive that, what a grand idea. I'd best be letting him know that we are in the process of rescuing your husband's machine and are going to see about rebuilding her." He continued "it'll be the longest letter I've writ in years, 'tis a fair ol' tale already."

In a very timely manner a Bradford Jowett van, advertising the Old White Hart Inn on its sides, was driven carefully onto the hangar apron. Jeannie jumped out from the passenger's seat almost before Charlie had gently brought the van to a halt. "Sandwiches and beer as ordered" she called out gaily to the hot and tired workers. Tools were quickly dropped, and a good natured scrummage developed at the back of the van where Charlie had opened the doors to reveal a keg of ale. Two large trays which were covered with snow white linen cloths were produced. The covers were removed to reveal sandwiches of ham, and cheese, plus cheese and ham. A jar of home-made apple chutney was also present on each tray. Charlie, feeling somewhat hemmed in shouted out "there's enough for all. Form an orderly queue. Blimy, anyone might think y' hadn't et fer a month ah Sundays." A voice from the back of the press called back, raising a laugh from the group, "never mind et'n, I'm that parched I could drink an oasis dry."

Valentine moved over to stand with Jasper, cheese and ham sandwich in one hand and glass tankard in the other, and asked "is this your doing?" "Aye lad, got to take care of the lads and lasses that's doing the hard labouring." Valentine replied "that's really generous of you Jasper but I can't let you stand the bill for all this. You won't be offended if I pay for half of it, will you?" Jasper smiled benignly saying, "nay lad, I'll not offended at all. Just as you won't be offended when I refuse your kind offer. Now get some of that good grub and another pot of ale down you; there's more than enough work to be done before nightfall."

So it was that they drifted back to their tasks refreshed and rested with a determination to have all the crates out to the front of the hangar before dusk set in. Giles, realising the bulk and weight of most of the crates would make it hard for them to be lifted and carried out by hand had coopted one of the farm hands to rig a shear-legs in the back of the Land Rover. It was made using three strong larch poles lashed near the top with rope. The two outer poles of the structure were wedged against the backboard of the cab and the sidewalls of the load-bed. These stood almost vertically, the middle leg was pulled back to be placed centrally against the tailgate. A block and tackle was suspended from the lashing at the apex of the shear-legs which in turn supported a longer larch pole that was mounted with one third of its length over the load-bed, and two thirds sticking out over the cab of the vehicle forming a jib. The inboard end of the crane jib was lashed to the central pole of the shear-legs. The butt end was positioned just below the top of the tailgate and a transverse pole was placed across the rear of the load bed side walls, this was also lashed to the middle pole of the shear-legs and tied down to the vehicle chassis. This arrangement prevented the butt end of the jib pole from rising when the heavy crates were being lifted. Using an over-cab jib would throw the weight of the load onto the front of the Land Rover providing stable platform whilst the loads were being drawn out from the back of the hangar. Giles' foresight in rigging his makeshift crane paid off as the crates were able to be lifted and pulled clear of the hay without every last forkful being cleared away. With all the crates now accessible Giles decided to call it night, even though the sun had yet to set. His cry of "to the pub lads" was echoed by all. They deserved a pint, or two, after the exertions of the day.

They enjoyed an evening of good company recounting stories of wartime events, both happy and sad. They spoke of their friends and families as Jane and Valentine became drawn into a deepening friendship with Jasper, Giles, Charlie, and the farm hands who had started to share in the enthusiasm that Val and Jane had for the project to rescue and restore Alex's little warplane. Jeannie was also drawn into the socializing and kept finding herself watching, and listening, to Valentine with an increasing sense of attraction. The socializing went on long into the evening, Charlie called 'time' and closed the bar, but the friends stayed talking about the adventure that was unfolding before them. Charlie kept filling their glasses, asserting that they were a private party, and they were his guests. "Well," he said with a grin "that's what I'll tell Constable Trigg if he comes calling to check up on me for serving after licencing hours are up."

Chapter 14

Rebirth

Early the following morning a not so bright Valentine dragged himself bleary eyed, and with a sore head, from his bed. Once his ablutions were completed he dressed in readiness for the tasks of un-crating his father's aeroplane and attempting to complete inventories of was, or wasn't, fit for re-use.

Jane intercepted him as he entered the kitchen bidding him a cheery "good morning darling." He tried to smile in return, but the effect was more akin to a grimace. With a wry smile Jane said, "The home brewed a bit heavier than you thought? Never mind, a good breakfast and a swift drive to the airfield will blow the cobwebs away. I thought porridge followed by a boiled egg and a slice of toast with a nice pot of tea should set you up after last night." Valentine pulled a face but accepted the food, knowing that his mother had his best interests at heart.

Breakfast over, the plates and cups washed and put away in the kitchen cupboards, they set off to the former airfield in Jane's immaculate open top sports tourer. The car was her pride and joy, after her beloved son of course. She drove with flair, skill, and panache navigating the country roads and lanes at speed but never recklessly so. As she had predicted the drive had 'blown the cobwebs away' by the time they drew up at the five barred gates which blocked the way onto the field. Someone must have got there before them since the gates were closed although they were not padlocked as they had been when Valentine first discovered the site. Valentine jumped out of the car, opened the gates and ushered his mother through before reclosing them and then jogging up the roadway to the perimeter track and on to the now busy hangar apron.

The whole team was raring to get stuck into the task of opening the crates to discover what treasures they might hold. Val and Giles were even more keen to start cataloguing the parts and sorting them out to determine where the various components would fit on, and into, the fuselage to recreate the aircraft. Giles had to take charge very firmly to ensure that the boxes were opened cautiously and the contents unpacked in a methodical and careful manner. He insisted that the boxes must be marked up so that each could be positively identified, and a contents list affixed to each in turn. Val had the foresight to bring his camera and several spare rolls of film with him. He insisted that each box and the components within them were photographed so that they had a record of everything that they recovered, and evidence of the condition of each component as it was removed from the packing and wrappings. His first task was to photograph the airframe and the wings. Once that task was complete he was ready for the crates and boxes, which had been spread around the apron on tarpaulin sheets to keep the contents as clean as possible as they were unpacked and inspected. Giles was all for lifting the engine out of its crate and checking it over for signs of damage and corrosion whilst Val took photographs at his direction.

Jasper, although just as keen as anyone else on site, decided that there were too many hands available, and most would spend much of their time watching what others were doing. He strode over to Giles and stated, "for the rest of the morning I'm tekin' most of the farm hands off to do some real work: whilst you, Val, Jane, and young Freddy there stay to do the boring stuff unpacking the bits and pieces and what-have-you." Freddy, needless to say, was overjoyed that he was being given the privilege of helping Giles and Val with the aeroplane. He had a love of all things mechanical and idolised Giles for his skills in maintaining, making do and mending the farm equipment.

Freddy Taylor was a lanky, tousle haired, young lad with a ready smile and a typical youngster's sense of mischief. He had that ability to look as if 'butter wouldn't melt in his mouth.' When behaving in a little too carefree a manner he was sometimes described as being a 'gormless yard of pump water.' Despite that he was actually a bright lad, prepared to pull his weight, and capable of much more than a labourer's life. He had recently finished his school days and had approached Giles one day when he was in the village to ask if there could be some work for him on the farm. Giles quickly took to the lad and, after speaking to Jasper about hiring him, he joined the team at Manor Farm as, in Giles' terminology, a 'gopher.' He was going to put heart and soul into helping Val and Giles put the old aeroplane back together and secretly hoped that he would be rewarded with a flight in it once it was done.

Jane was placed in charge of the clerical work cataloguing the parts and making sure that Val did not take any photographs of components that had not first been labelled, and that the details on the labels were visible when the photographs were taken. The catalogued parts were rewrapped and placed back in their respective boxes and crates ready for attention when needed. They hardly stopped for the lunch which, as before, was delivered to them by Jeannie who stayed with them for quite a while quietly watching Val as he went about his photography. She was intrigued to see him checking light levels and setting up the various subjects for his photographs so that the details were brought out by the natural light. She caught him trying to catch a picture of her unawares, which made her giggle and strike a pose for his camera.

At the end of the day everything was packed away. The crates and boxes were covered with the tarpaulins. Giles reluctantly had to place the engine back in its cradle and move it into the old hangar before covering it to prevent the dew from settling on it overnight. The fuselage was left out, it wouldn't come to any harm from the weather overnight as their principal task for the following day would be to strip down the fuselage to its bare bones.

Val and Jane were on site bright and early even beating Giles and Freddy to the start of the day's work. They set about stripping away the old fabric, taking great care with the section close to the tail where the aircraft's service serial, TW348, was painted. Val had decided on the previous day that he would preserve that part of the original by having it cleaned and mounted in a glazed picture frame. The old doped Irish linen came away quite easily. The bare bones of the tubular steel fuselage upon which the wooden formers and stringers, which gave aerodynamic shape to the fuselage over the boxy airframe structure, were affixed were soon revealed. The formers and stringers were found to be in exceptionally good condition and it looked like they could be re-used once they had been cleaned, checked for defects, and varnished. The wire clips that retained the stringers to the formers together with the pressed steel tabs which held the formers onto the fuselage tubes, and the screws which secured them, were lightly corroded. Valentine left the removal of the woodwork, and the metal clips, to be undertaken once Giles arrived.

When Giles appeared with young Freddy on the pillion of his pre-war Douglas motorbike Val had already started to remove the cockpit doors. Once they were detached from the airframe Freddy was given the job of removing the fabric from them before removing the flat acrylic glazing panels that formed the 'slide to open' windows, and the door latch mechanisms. Giles and Val set about the fiddly job of removing the screws that secured the windscreen, rear cockpit side and top glazing panels, and the forward section of the canopy to the wooden frames that were in their turn fastened to the tubular framework of the aircraft. This took longer than they originally expected since some of the screws holding the frames in place were heavily corroded and had to be drilled out, with much cursing, using a hand cranked pinion drill. During this bit of work Valentine raised the question of the retaining clips and tabs from the stringers and formers with Giles. "They might be usable again when cleaned up" remarked Valentine but Giles voiced his opinion saying "they would be easy to replace with new. So why penny-pinch?" Once that decision was made they set about removing the stringers and formers. Each one was carefully numbered and its position on the fuselage was recorded to ensure that they were replaced exactly in the positions from which they were removed when the rebuilding work was undertaken.

The seat frames, and the armour plate beneath the Pilot's seat which had been scarred by several machine gun bullets that would otherwise have killed Alex Shooter instantly, were the next to be removed by Val who had designated himself as the 'cockpit man'. Jane was given the role of photographer and note-taker in chief, she meticulously gave each piece a unique identity before it was photographed and catalogued.

Their next job was to draw out the thin steel wire cables that connected the flying controls to the rudder, elevator, trim tab, ailerons, also the cables from the heel operated brake pedals, and the car style handbrake lever, to main-wheel brakes, Val disconnected these in the cockpit for Freddy to pull them clear and catalogue them with Jane.

The electrical wiring for the battery, ground power socket, electric starter motor, wind driven dynamo, navigation lights, recognition lights, the radio equipment, and engine instrumentation would also have to be stripped out: as would the tubing associated with the pitot head and venturi tube from which the pressure driven blind flying panel instruments were driven. Finally, before the instrument panel sections and their mounting frame could be removed it was necessary to disconnect the throttle, fuel mixture, 'ki-gas' primer pump, and carburettor heat control plungers from the sub-panel in which they were mounted on the centre of the lower edge of the main instrument panel structure. This provided easy access to the wiring and pressure tubing that was located behind the instrument panel. The panel was made in two pieces mounted on a tubular frame across the cockpit. There were several inches of clearance from the rear of the fuel tank, which sat immediately below the windscreen, on the cockpit side of the firewall. The blind flying panel was mounted on the left side of the cockpit in front of the Pilot. The various light switches and connectors for the army 22 set, a high frequency radio, were positioned on the right-hand part of the panel where both the Pilot and observer could reach them.

Master Sergeant Joe Kennedy had taken care of the bulky 'P' type magnetic compass when he had prepared the airplane for storage. That fragile instrument had been carefully packed away in its own made to measure plywood case that had been clearly marked 'FRAGILE HANDLE WITH CARE.' The fuel tank, gascolator, fuel lines and fuel shut-off cock also had to be removed, a task made easier with the seats out of the way.

Each task was recorded, photographs were taken, and sketches made where it was thought that re-assembly might be made easier if they had some drawings to which they could refer. The whole exercise of reducing the airframe to its constituent parts took them three days during which Giles was fretting about getting on with the inspection of the engine and test running it as soon as he was satisfied that it was in good order. He kept saying "I need the Land Rover and the engine is still hanging from our crane." In reality he just wanted to start tinkering with it. Val had to rein him in telling him that the engine could not be touched until it had been registered, and then all the work would have to be done under the supervision of, and signed off by, a Board of Trade Licenced Engineer qualified to undertake work on aircraft power plants.

With Jane in charge of the paperwork she had wasted little time finding out what needed to be done to have the aeroplane registered with the Board of Trade as a privately owned machine on the Civil Aircraft Register whilst carrying the original military markings that it wore when flown by her husband. Thankfully her education, particularly at Cambridge and her subsequent service as an Officer in the FANY, stood her in good stead for the challenges of dealing with the Civil Service bureaucracy that was to follow.

Nobody was prepared for the obstacles that were going to be placed in their way for returning the former RAF Auster Mark V aircraft to the skies in civilian ownership whilst being presented in her original D-Day warpaint, carrying her original RAF serial number of TW348, and the identification letters for 659 Squadron. Jane addressed her first letter to the Aircraft Registration Board at the Board of Trade setting out her request for the aeroplane to be taken onto the British Civil Register of Aeroplanes. This would be first document in what would grow into a file having as many pages as moderately sized book. Her letter was simple and succinct.

Holly Cottage,
Church Lane,
Middle Down,
West Sussex.

Aircraft Registration Board,
Board of Trade,
55 Kingsway
London WC2

Dear Sir

Civil registration of a former military aircraft: Auster Mk V

We are in possession of an Auster Mk V aeroplane which was formerly on RAF charge as TW348. The manufacturer's serial number is 3379. The aircraft is now owned by Mr. G Chamberlain of Manor Farm, Upham, West Sussex.

It is our intention to operate the aeroplane for our personal and private use only. Therefore, we believe a Private Category Certificate of Airworthiness would be appropriate.

The aeroplane was flown by my late husband in an AOP role in Normandy during the last war and it is our wish that it be restored with the same military camouflage and markings carried at the time of his demise in August 1944.

Please provide me with the necessary and sufficient forms required to place this aeroplane on the civil register. I would be most grateful for any advice as may be appropriate leading to us flying the aeroplane in in the military markings as described.

Yours Faithfully

J Shooter (Mrs)
25th. August 1967

Suffice to say the response from a Mr R Thompson displayed neither of those attributes. His response was stiffly formal, long winded, although businesslike. The style remained the same in every letter that Jane received from him over the following months. He set out a number of requirements, Jane viewed them as demands, the first of which required Mr G Chamberlain to furnish proof of ownership supported by a Certificate of Release from the Air Ministry relating to the aeroplane in question. Mr Thompson made it quite clear that until such documentation had been provided and authenticated the application for civil registration would not be progressed.

Not having any such paperwork, Jane responded advising Mr Thompson that the aeroplane had been abandoned at the former USAAF station RAF Upham Manor and had been included in an all-encompassing bill of sale when the land, together with the buildings and contents therein, was restored to the pre-war owners from who it had been requisitioned at start of the War: namely the Chamberlain family. The result was a protracted exchange of correspondence punctuated by personal visits, made by both Jane and Giles either individually or together over a period of many months, for meetings with various civil servants of increasing seniority as time progressed. The first meeting in London was arranged to determine provenance. That meeting was attended by Jane and Giles, Mr Thompson, and several other people from the Board of Trade, plus interested parties from the Air Ministry and the War Department. The combined body of civil servants expressed concern that valuable military equipment had found its way into civilian hands. Furthermore, they demanded that said equipment be returned to the Air Ministry for proper disposal. Once the chairborne warriors had finally exhausted their indignation, and had settled into frosty silence, Giles pointed out that the airframe was unarmed and derelict. It had been effectively destroyed by enemy action in nineteen forty-four and that the dismantled aircraft had been stored by the USAAF until their tenure of the airfield had ceased in nineteen forty-six. Furthermore, it had remained in storage during the period when the airfield was placed on a 'Care and Maintenance' basis by Royal Air Force and had been abandoned when the RAF moved off the land in nineteen forty-eight. The disused airfield, and everything associated with the site that had not been removed by the Royal Air Force, had been offered for sale to the family business in nineteen forty-eight. They, under the terms of the Requisition Order of nineteen forty, had the right of first refusal to buy back the land. The title to the land was thereby passed back to his family. Furthermore, the Deed of Transfer incorporated title to the buildings and the contents thereof. He expressed his opinion, rather forcefully, stating "if the RAF is correct in their claim to ownership of the derelict and dismantled aircraft Manor Farm Limited would be obliged to raise an invoice for storage charges in respect of it." This statement produced much 'huffing and puffing' with phrases like 'the Government will not be held to ransom' and 'most unpatriotic' being heard from the ranks of the administrative civil servants present. The effect upon the meeting as a whole was to the great amusement of both Giles and Jane. Giles, decided to appear more conciliatory and went on to suggest that the Operational Record Books for RAF Upham Manor would almost certainly reveal the date and time of arrival of Auster aircraft TW348. He doubted that the USAAF records, if any were to be made available, would indicate what action had subsequently been taken to return the aircraft to the RAF. He argued his case saying, "whilst there was no specific inventory associated with the Deed of Transfer relating to the land, the buildings and sundry materiel stored therein, there could be little doubt that the Courts would uphold his family's claim to the derelict airframe now to be legally in their possession."

Some weeks later Jane received another letter from Mr Thompson, rather pompously worded she thought, in which it was conceded that the derelict aircraft serial TW348 was in fact owned by Mr Chamberlain. Jane was not one to 'let the grass grow under her feet' and spent the period between the Christmas and New Year celebrations working her way through the paperwork which she and Val had regarded as a wonderful Christmas present. The application to register ownership in the joint names of Giles Chamberlain of Manor Farm, Upham, West Sussex, and Valentine Shooter of Holly Cottage, Middle Down, West Sussex, together with the application for civil registration were winging their way back to Mr Thompson's desk from the mail room at Cranfield University on Monday the eighth of January nineteen sixty-eight.

After reading through the requirements for the issue of the Private Category C of A Giles called Val on the 'phone and raged about the conditions that they would have to satisfy. He was particularly annoyed about the conditions regarding the engine, which he saw as his 'baby.' "They are insisting that the engine has to be completely stripped and rebuilt to an 'as new' specification by a Licenced Aircraft Engineer and signed off by a separate Licenced Engineer who has piston engines on his ticket." He ranted "that means I can't touch the bloody thing!" Val tried to sooth him down, and reminding Giles of what he had told him months before when they first removed the engine from its storage crate. However, that didn't do anything to help matters either. Val suggested that Giles contact people at Shoreham Airport where one of the Beagle factories was situated. He pointed out that the Auster company had been merged with other businesses to form British Executive & General Aviation Limited; the Headquarters of which were at Shoreham Airport, not all that far from Upham. Val suggested that Giles might be able to persuade them to let him work on the engine under the supervision of their engineers; thereby ensuring the engine would be signed off as being 'zero timed' whilst the costs would be kept to a minimum by Giles doing the actual work under the banner of the Beagle company as they were known.

Giles made contact by telephone with the Chief Engineer at the Shoreham factory that afternoon and a meeting at the factory was arranged for the Tuesday of the following week. Giles turned up for that meeting full of confidence. However, he was soon knocked back slightly when the Engine Shop Foreman, Teddy Neale, pointed out the engine was an American Lycoming 0-290 air cooled flat four and that whilst they carried out maintenance work on that type of engine it was usual for them to return complete units to the American factory for re-build. Nevertheless, he understood the situation and accepted, that since Giles was a former REME man with a wealth of experience where engines were concerned, they might find a way to get round the problem. So it was that a somewhat deflated Giles made his way back to Manor Farm from where he would make a call to Val in Cranfield with the not so pleasing news.

Deciding to bite the bullet, Giles rode over to Shoreham on his motorcycle a few days later to make arrangements for Beagle to send the engine off to America. At the reception desk he asked if Teddy Neale was available for an informal chat. Teddy was paged over the works Tannoy system, and he arrived in the reception area after about a quarter of an hour. He greeted Giles warmly and, with a grin, said "Giles old son, we think we've come up with a work around regarding your engine." Giles face immediately broke out with a wide smile, "really Teddy," he said, "what's the plan?"

"Well, you said the aircraft was in action in Normandy and brought its dying Pilot home in early August nineteen forty-four. I've done a bit of ferreting around in the Auster company records and found that the batch of Austers with engines in that run of serial numbers wasn't issued to the RAF until the middle of July nineteen forty-four. We haven't got access to the RAF maintenance records so we don't know for sure how many hours were put on the engine; but I doubt that it clocked fifty hours absolute tops. So, provided that it has been properly stored it should be as good as new inside. I've asked the Chief Engineer at the Auster Factory at Rearsby up in Leicestershire and our resident ARB Inspector if we can issue a Certificate of Compliance if we, you and I, strip it to check all the parts for compliance with the as new dimensions and condition before using them for zero hours rebuild. Of course, any components that fail inspection will have to be scrapped and brand-new parts fitted. All the parts, reused and new, will have Certificates of Compliance and we'll get it signed it off for you." Giles could barely contain himself. The first thing he said was "when can we start?" "Hold your horses" Teddy said. "We need to set up a proper Work Order number and Scheme of Work before we start getting ahead of ourselves. I'll drop you a line once we're ready to go. Also, the 'Governor' has asked to see you."

Teddy led Giles from his shop floor office back to the receptionist's desk and asked if the 'Governor' was free to see Mr Chamberlain. The young lady said, "I'll check for you" as picked up a handset whilst keying a switch on the console of her internal telephone system. She spoke to tell her boss that his visitors had arrived, then listened with a slight frown on her face. She replaced the handset on its cradle, whilst flipping the console switch back to its previous position. She looked up at Giles, smiled and said "The Chairman apologises for not being able to meet you at present. He is unavoidably detained with an urgent matter. He has asked Sir Henry Milner, the Board Member for Special Projects, to see you in his stead. Sir Henry is awaiting you in the Boardroom now sir. Mr Neale will take you up." Teddy ushered Giles up the stairs to where the Design, Production, Purchasing and Accountants' offices were situated on either side of a long corridor. This led to a large, polished, door at the far end. Teddy knocked and opened the door immediately; a secretary sat at a desk directly in front of the pair as they entered. The very smartly attired lady rose from her chair and welcomed them to the Chairman's Office and the Boardroom. She turned and trapped on the door to the left of her desk as they faced it. Opening the door to its fullest extent she announced, "Mr Chamberlain and Mr Neale are here for you Sir Henry." The man who had been seated at the head of a large mahogany table, around which a dozen plushly upholstered chairs were set, rose and extended his hand to Giles. He spoke in a soft, cultured but authoritarian, voice saying "Mr Chamberlain, how good of you to come up to see me. Please take a seat, you too Mr Neale." He indicated two chairs next to his at the head of the table: "Shirley please would you bring us a tray, tea or coffee, Mr Chamberlain, Mr Neale?" "Oh! Tea please" was the response from both the visitors. "I am Henry Milner a member of the Board of Directors of the Beagle group of companies" said their host as he sat down in his chair. "The Chairman and the members of the Board heard about your need for a zero timed Lycoming that has come to you in rather unusual circumstances, we'd like to know more?"

Giles was slightly taken aback by the interest from such an eminent man, but he started by telling Sir Henry that it was a long story and asking if he wanted the short version. "Let me hear it all" responded Sir Henry just as Shirley returned with the tea tray which she set down in the centre of the table, in front of the trio, before pouring the tea for the three of them. Sugar, milk, and a plateful of assorted biscuits was also provided with the tea. Having ascertained the guests' requirement for either sugar or milk she handed round the brimming cups and then asked, "will that be all Sir Henry?" He replied, "Yes, thank you Shirley: and Shirley" he paused for a second or two before continuing "we are not to be disturbed for quite some time I think."

With the almost silent closing of the Boardroom door Giles launched into the story of Alex Shooter's fateful last operational flight in Normandy and the remarkable arrival of the Auster back at RAF Upham Manor with its dead and dying crew. He told of Joe Kennedy's careful stripping down and storage arrangements for the aircraft in readiness for the RAF to take it away. He continued with the story telling of the crated aircraft being left behind when the USAAF pulled out and of the return of the airfield to the RAF on a 'care and maintenance' basis. He continued his narrative explaining that the RAF hadn't taken much notice of what the Americans had left behind, and that the RAF had closed the station when the land was sold back to his family, complete with all that was built on the land and the contents of the buildings. He finished the story by telling of Valentine's strange quest, his discovery of the old aircraft stored behind the haystack in the former hanger, and of their plans to rebuild the aircraft as a living memorial to Valentine's father and his AOP comrades who had flown their little unarmed aircraft into battle.

Sir Henry had sat quietly as Giles had told the story and continued to do so for a quite few moments after Giles had finished speaking, obviously deep in thought before reaching for the teapot offering his guests a refill and pouring a fresh cupful for himself. "I have never been so enthralled by a story as I have whilst listening to yours. It's quite amazing and the plans for the future of the aircraft are a wonderful idea. I can only say that we at Beagle will do all we can to assist you and your friends in your endeavours. Our team at Beagle-Auster will provide you with whatever advice you will need from time to time, and we here at Shoreham will provide any physical assistance that you require on a not-for-profit basis. How does that sound to you?"

Giles was lost for words but managed to say, "thank you, thank you very much, I never expected so generous an offer." He went on to say, "one bit of advice I need quite urgently relates to getting the work done by Licenced Engineers and does that have to be at a factory, or workshop, that is approved by the ARB?" "That's a good question and I think Mr Neale will be able to give you the answers you require" said Sir Henry. He added "I believe Mr Neale has told you about the situation with your engine and I can assure you that we will find a way of keeping the ARB Inspectors on our side." Teddy Neale joined the conversation saying as far as the airframe was concerned, "I believe that we could allow you and your friend Mr Shooter to undertake all the preparatory work in your own workshop: and I will make sure that the Work Schedules together with the signed off Worksheets are kept here at Shoreham. I'm sure that both you, Mr Shooter, and your Apprentice can be trusted to work under our indirect supervision; but you will have to demonstrate that your work is up to the standards expected. We can make provision for the final erection work and the rigging of the controls to be done here at Shoreham." Sir Henry stood up indicating that the meeting was over, then he added, "we will also be able to arrange for one of our production test Pilots to undertake the necessary flight testing to satisfy the ARB that the aircraft will have been constructed to our factory standards such that it can be released to service." He smiled broadly as he said, "the bill won't be too great a strain on your pockets!" With that he ushered them to the door, thanking both Giles and Teddy Neale for their time and the pleasure of both hearing the story and of doing business with Giles.

A few days later, Giles had a telephone call from a pleasant-sounding chap who introduced himself as Jim Pearce from the Beagle-Auster works at Rearsby in Leicestershire. He told Giles that Sir Henry had asked him if would care to supervise the re-building and testing of an ex-RAF Auster Mark V that was now in civilian hands. He said that Sir Henry had told the whole story as Giles had told it to him. Jim was intrigued and more than keen to assist with the project. He asked Giles if it would be convenient for him to visit Upham in order to see the machine and get a feel for what would be required to get the aircraft back to flying condition. Giles asked him when he would like to come down to West Sussex, Jim replied "would this weekend be too soon?" Giles laughed, "not a minute too soon, and I'm sure that we can find you a bed for the night." "Right," responded Jim "I shall be at the Shoreham factory on Friday, I shall motor over once I've finished there if that will be OK with you and I'll head back home on Saturday evening when I have all the information I need about your aeroplane."

The following week a sizeable package, with Leicester postmarks, was delivered to Jane at Holly Cottage. Inside she found a letter from Jim Pearce in which he explained that he had pulled out copies of the building schedule for the AOP Mark V Auster and had amended it to reflect the situation relating to TW348. He enclosed the amended document together with Worksheets to cover all the tasks required to complete the amended schedule. He finished by stating that he estimated a minimum of three hundred man-hours of work would be needed, and quite probably more, to complete the work to the standards required for the issue of C of A.

A few days later the whole team got together in the Old White Hart; they all sat in the Smoke Room and over several pints of Charlie's best home brewed beer they sketched out a list of tasks that had to be completed. They also put together a plan of action to achieve their goal of getting the Auster back into the skies, registered as G-UNNR painted as TW348 of 659 Squadron RAF. Their initial list had the following headings:

1. full airframe inspection, including wings and empennage,
2. instrument overhauls and re-calibration,
3. instrument panel fitting,
4. new UHF radio fitout,
5. dynamo testing (overhaul if necessary) fitting into the starboard wing, wiring for dynamo,
6. battery carrier position in fuselage behind cockpit (battery fitting when aircraft ready for testing), power circuit wiring including ground power socket on port side fuselage,
7. fitting and rigging, wings, empennage and flying control surfaces,
8. rewiring electric circuits,
9. installation of pitot head and connecting tubing to instruments,
10. installation of venturi tubes and pipework to vacuum driven instruments,
11. installing cockpit flying controls,
12. fitting undercarriage, main wheels with tyres and tubes, tailwheel spring and tailwheel assembly,
13. installing firewall and firewall furniture,

14. fuel tank, check for internal rusting, clean and seal, replace (if necessary) pipework for fuel lines. Strip and overhaul (if needed) the fuel cock and fuel gascolator.
15. Engine mounts and engine installation, Starter motor,
16. Connection of engine controls, and instrumentation (oil pressure and temperature, cylinder head temperature)
17. Engine strip, reassemble and check compressions,
18. Engine runs – bedding in,
19. Propellor inspection and certification,
20. Cockpit glazing,
21. Seats – mil or civ?
22. Paint,
23. weight and balance.
24. Compass fitting – calibration * last item before test flt.
25. Anything else?

As the list grew so did the looks of concern of the faces of group. Jasper finally said, "that's a hell of a lot of work to do lads, is it viable?" "There's only one way to find out and that's to make an immediate start; well tomorrow anyhow, and do whatever we can whenever we can with the help of whoever we can rope in. Beagle have pledged their support and are willing to push to get the paperwork through as quickly as they can: and we have the Worksheets to check our progress and as proof of our work for the Engineers to sign off."

The aircraft had, at this stage, been reduced to a kit of parts. The paint on the tubular steel structures had been stripped away allowing them to be closely examined for signs of rusting and cracking. There were two areas in the cockpit where bullets had dented, and in one case pierced, the steel tubes. These, and the few slightly rusted areas found when closely examined, had been repaired using techniques that were approved by the Royal Air Force and Board of Trade. The steel tubular airframe, engine mounts, and empennage components had been stripped back to bare metal for the inspection and when declared to be compliant to the standards applicable had been coated in primer, before repainting in military olive drab. The engine bearers were treated differently from the other steel parts, they were painted in heat resistant black lacquer. The wooden wing spars had been cleaned, examined, and found to be free from defects. The completed airframe work was inspected by a pair of Licenced Engineers from Beagle's Shoreham factory and the required documentation signed off.

The engine parts had been taken to Teddy Neale's engine shop at Shoreham for inspection and testing. Much to Giles's relief they were found to be in perfect condition and within specified tolerances. The Certificates of Compliance were signed, and the engine was reassembled at Shoreham; a week later it ready for bench testing. The engine ran beautifully smoothly and was soon declared ready for return to Giles, complete with the pile of paperwork that attested as to its fitness for service, and for installation in the airframe once that was ready. Teddy had his Mechanic fill the engine with passivating fluid to protect it until the day came for mounting in the airframe. Giles was 'like a dog with two tails' when he collected 'his baby' from Teddy.

Whilst the wheels of bureaucracy were slowly grinding toward an acceptance that his dad's Auster could be returned to the skies Val, along with Jane and Freddy Taylor, carried out as much preparatory work as could be done to the airframe, wings and flying control surfaces. Val was away at Cranfield University much of the time undertaking the work towards his Doctorate, but he was home every weekend to work on the Auster: Jeannie managed to spend most of her free time with Val whilst he was there helping where she could. She was also working hard at fostering a strong romantic attachment, to which Val responded quite readily, a fact that didn't go unnoticed by Jane who thoroughly approved without saying so outright.

Giles and young Freddy put in as much time working through the tasks that Jim had listed on the Worksheets as they could when they were able to get away from essential farmwork. Accepting Jim's advice Giles concentrated on the airframe and put aside the engine until they had made enough progress to warrant preparing the newly certified engine for mounting on the airframe. Weeks, and months, passed with steady progress being made. As each Worksheet was completed Giles invited Jim to have the work checked and signed off by one of the Licenced Engineers from the Shoreham factory. Jim called in to see for himself how the work was progressing and, on each occasion, expressed his delight at the high standards of workmanship they were producing.

Both Val and Giles were worried about re-covering the fuselage and the wings with Irish linen since they had no previous experience of working with the fabric and no knowledge of the techniques required. They had no idea of the approved methods for securing the fabric to the wooden stringers and formers which they had affixed to the newly rust proofed and repainted tubular steel fuselage, or to the ribs and spars of the wing and aileron structures. These tasks were further complicated by the need to provide inspection access panels at certain locations on the fuselage and the wings. Those on the fuselage were triangular areas zipped along two sides those on the wings were circular openings which were completely covered by fabric patches. Giles raised the matter with Jim during one of his visits to the hanger.

Jim agreed that it would be a task beyond their abilities and after a period of reflection he suggested that they might try to get some guidance and hands on help from an experienced fabric worker who had recently retired from the Beagle-Miles Shoreham factory. He said "I have nobody specifically in mind because I haven't had any direct dealings with the Fabric Shop there; I know a couple of people who used to work at the Rearsby Factory who might be induced to take a working holiday down here with you to get the job done. I'll ask around and see if anyone would be willing to come over to teach you how it's done, and make sure that the job's done right."

Two weeks later a letter arrived for Giles from a couple who had worked at the Rearsby factory, the wife was an experienced fabric worker and the husband an airframe rigger. They said that Jimpee had contacted them with a suggestion that they might like to take a working holiday in West Sussex all expenses paid in exchange for help with the restoration of the Auster Mark V, which both knew well and had probably been involved with its original manufacture, rigging and preparation for RAF service. They were called Stephen and Catherine Weston. They said that they had no ties that would prevent them from spending a few weeks in West Sussex, and they could be there as soon as Giles could accommodate them and set them to work. Jane wrote back immediately thanking them for their wonderful offer to help them put her late husband's aeroplane back into an airworthy condition and offering to have them stay with her at Holly cottage. The Westons replied saying that they would arrive by car in the late afternoon of the Monday following, if that was alright with Mrs Shooter. Jane dropped them a quick note thanking them again for their willingness to come down to stay with her and to teach the team how to handle the difficult task of getting the fabric covering on the aeroplane. She said that afternoon tea would be ready for them when they arrived. She concluded her note with a little sketch map showing them the route they should take after they left Midhurst on the A286 towards Chichester.

Once the Westons arrived and had looked over the airframe, wing, and control surfaces they sat down with Jane and Jeannie, who by then was taking a real interest in her sweetheart's aeroplane, to work out a plan of attack for the fabric work. Cath, as she preferred to be called, had suggested when they first discussed the project that they use the latest man-made fabric. Whilst it wasn't strictly in accordance with the original build Ceconite 102 would be easier to work with and using it with modern two-pack paints, instead of coloured dopes, would produce a more robust finish. Meanwhile, Giles had been in contact with the Production Manager at Shoreham to ask if he could supply him with a quantity of a suitable grade of aircraft fabric sufficient to recover the Auster with 'a bit to spare' in case of accidents or mistakes. The Stores Manager at Beagle strongly supported Cath's decision and changed the order from Irish linen to Ceconite: he pointed out that it was also cheaper to buy.

In due course a large package was delivered to the farm which contained a bale of Ceconite 102 fabric, which had been approved for use, instead of the heavier and less durable Irish linen. There were a couple of bobbins of rib lacing cord, packets of drain grommets, and several spools of tapes for various applications which included self-adhesive anti-chafing, reinforcing, rib-bracing, and surface tapes: all with the necessary Certificates of Compliance for the individual materials. The bill for the materials supplied was also enclosed. Also included was note reminding Giles that he would also have to order the necessary glue, fabric sealant dope, fillers, and paints to complete the job. Giles rang the factory number to order the additional materials, which arrived two days later.

Cath told the group who would be working with her and her husband, "you must start small and simple." The tailplanes, elevators, and rudder were the simplest frameworks since there were no internal aerofoil ribs with which to contend. These parts were approximately triangular with rounded corners. The port side elevator was a little more complex since a hinged trim-tab, connected to the trimming control handle in the cockpit by a control wire, was mounted in the trailing edge of the control surface. The cockpit doors were also very simple to cover being almost flat structures of trapezoidal shape. Jane and Jeannie laid the tubular structures onto a length of ceconite fabric and cut out the required shapes using very large tailors shears that Cath had brought with her. Cath showed them how, and where, to attach the necessary tapes that would protect the ceconite and strengthen the joints in the fabric covering. They did several 'dry runs' to familiarise themselves with the way in the fabric moved and reacted to being stretched and tensioned before they committed to gluing the fabric to the framework. With the fabric in place the most challenging task in the re-covering process remained; the ceconite had to be tensioned using a hot smoothing iron. Cath undertook this work herself. However, she did take time to teach both Jane and Jeannie how to do the work to produce a tight wrinkle free finish ready for painting. Whilst the preparations for applying the new fabric covering had been going ahead Giles was busy with Teddy Neale undertaking the necessary inspection work for certification and the signing off of the work that had been done. Teddy was most impressed and found absolutely nothing to criticize. He went as far as to joke "keep this up and Beagle will be sub-contracting work to Manor Farm Aviation unlimited."

Steven, Stevie as he preferred to be known, told them that it would make life much easier later on if they ran pull cords through the fairleads in the frames to which control surfaces would be attached and to make the same provision for the electrical wiring to the taillight that would be fitted the rudder. He also made the same suggestion for the control wire runs, electrical wiring, and vacuum system tubing that ran through the wings and fuselage. That weekend Val installed all the control wires and wiring, the latter he laced up into looms once all the wires were in place with sufficient spare to make termination easy and to allow for some repositioning of the kit to which the wires would be attached.

The question of which radio fit would be installed had to be determined since the army 22 set was now obsolete and did not work over the civil aviation frequency band of 118 to 137 Mhz. The most up-to-date vhf air-band radio was self-evidently not in keeping with a restoration of the aircraft exactly as flown by Alex Shooter but would make operating the aircraft as a civil aircraft when visiting modern airports, and the larger civil or military airfields, where it was essential for the Pilots operating in the locality to be contact with Air Traffic Control. For situational awareness it was also important for the Pilots to be able to hear the calls to and from other aircraft operating in the area. They would also need a range of crystals to swap over for frequencies used elsewhere. They quickly discounted this option as being too restrictive and decided that a larger thirty-six channel set would be fitted for to give them the flexibility needed on longer trips. The larger set would not fit into the panel area, in front of the right-hand seat, without protruding from the panel by an inch or so due to lack of space. The nose-mounted fuel tank, which was positioned above the Pilot's knees, took up most of the space between the firewall and the back of the instrument panel. Whilst deliberating which radio, if any, was to be fitted it occurred to Val that they would have to obtain a Radio Licence from the Office of the Postmaster General. Jane's skills relating to dealing with bureaucracy were again called upon. Thankfully, this proved to be a very straightforward application. However, there was a sting in the tail: the details of the radio transceiver would have to be registered and the installation would have to have a Certificate of Compliance signed off by a Licenced Radio Engineer proficient in the installation and testing of aviation band transmitters. The radio had yet to be bought and installation was scheduled for some time in the future.

Jane's brother, Ollie Squires, had survived the war and continued to serve as decorated and well-respected Officer in the much-reduced postwar army. With the reorganisation of the airborne forces in nineteen fifty-seven Major Squires DFC RA had opted to transfer permanently from his parent Royal Artillery Regiment to the newly created Army Air Corps. It had been a difficult decision to make. The new Corps was a small and elite organisation that offered little or no prospect of promotion for a substantive Major. Nevertheless, the call of the skies was more demanding than that of attaining high rank as a Gunner. Ollie's current posting was to the AAC headquarters at Middle Wallop in Hampshire which gave him opportunities to visit Jane and Val quite often. When Alex's Auster had been found in Jasper's former hanger he had taken a keen interest in developments. He was especially supportive of the aircraft being returned to an airworthy condition as a tribute both to Alex and the aircrew of the wartime AOP Squadrons. He was disappointed that the ARB had, in his view, taken a stuffy attitude to the aircraft being fully restored in its D-Day Squadron markings. He had a firm resolve to 'see about that' and started a campaign within the AAC to obtain a formal waiver from complete compliance with the requirement for the civil aviation registration letters to be visible on the surfaces of the wings and fuselage. Ollie badgered his Commanding Officer, and when opportunity presented other Senior Officers, to help his nephew to display his late father's aircraft in the camouflage scheme and markings that it wore when Captain Shooter was killed in action. He was very persuasive in selling the idea that the aircraft would be a fitting flying memorial to Captain Shooter MC RA and all the men who served in the AOP Squadrons in World War Two, as well as in more recent operations. His persistence bore fruit when the Chief of the Army Staff got behind the proposal and spoke to the Chief of the Air Staff. The later wrote to the Secretary of State for Air and his approval was eventually granted. Alex's Auster would be exempt from the requirement to display civil aviation markings and would be identified by its former RAF serial number and the Squadron markings that it carried in Normandy in nineteen forty-four. A curt letter signed by Mr Thompson was received from Aircraft Registration Board. It read:

Aircraft Registration Board,
Board of Trade,
55 Kingsway
London WC2

Our reference: ARB/CR/BAL3379/rt
Your reference:
Date: 12th July 1968

Mrs J Shooter
Holly Cottage,
Church Lane,
Middledown,
West Sussex.
Dear Madam,

Civil Registration Auster Mk V manufacturer's serial number 3379.

Further to our previous correspondence regarding the display of the assigned civil registration markings on the wings and fuselage of the above-mentioned aeroplane I am directed to advise you that agreement has been made at the highest levels for those specific requirements to be waived in these exceptional circumstances. This exceptional authorisation shall apply to the aforementioned aeroplane and none other.

The aeroplane may be flown within the boundaries of the United Kingdom of Great Britain and Northern Ireland carrying the operational markings of Number 659 Squadron of The Royal Air Force and the serial number of TW348.

I am further directed to advise you that the aeroplane may not be exported whilst carrying Royal Air Force markings except for the purpose of specifically authorised flights outwith those boundaries. Permission from national aviation bodies of the countries to be visited must also be gained in writing prior to any such private flights being undertaken.

Yours faithfully

R Thompson,
Senior Registration Officer

Much to Jane's surprise there was a second letter in the envelope. It was and written on a single sheet of good quality notepaper.

Dear Mrs Shooter,

I am putting aside my official persona to thank you personally for the manner in which both you and Mr Chamberlain have addressed this most difficult of negotiations.

I have been impressed by the tenacity and level headedness displayed in our meetings when so much appeared to be in opposition to your objectives. It is with heartfelt pleasure that I am the bearer of the good tidings set out in my official letter enclosed.

12/07/68

There had been some discussion in the aviation press regarding participation in the celebrations which were in an advanced state of planning by the British, French and other allied countries to mark the Twenty-fifth anniversary of the liberation of France following the allied invasion over the beaches of Normandy in nineteen forty-four. Over a few pints and supper in the Smoke Room at the Old White Hart Inn in Upham the group of friends that had been brought together by Valentine's mysterious quest to 'find it' the idea was floated that if they made a herculean effort, they could have TW348 ready to take to France as a special salute to the AOP Squadrons and the dangerous work that they had carried out. They resolved to fulfil the dream that had been born on the day Valentine has discovered his late father's aeroplane.

It was agreed that Valentine and Giles would crew the Auster for the visit. Jane, ever practical, reminded them of the strictures placed upon the temporary export of the aircraft and foresaw a mountain of paperwork and official prevarication. "If we are going to go off to France to celebrate with everyone else, we must get our skates on; officialdom won't hurry themselves and we could easily 'miss the boat'. Oops sorry almost a pun there." She laughed; the others joined in merrily. Good as her word she started the letter writing with one to the Air Registration Board seeking permission for the temporary export of G-UNNR to France for private purposes during a period, as yet to be exactly specified, between fourth and fourteenth of June nineteen sixty-nine. She also wrote to the French Air Ministry requesting permission to fly in French airspace in an Auster aeroplane having a civil registration of G-UNNR but presented in a paint scheme used by the Royal Air Force during the operations in Normandy in nineteen forty-four. To provide some moral support she spoke to her brother Ollie asking him if he could 'gee up their airships' in the Air Ministry to expedite matters. Ollie told her "on the assumption that Val would be 'champing at the bit' to go and represent the AOP Squadrons I have already raised the matter with them. The Officer Commanding the Army Air Corps and the General Officer Commanding Airborne Forces are whole heartedly behind us." Caught in a pincer movement between Jane and Ollie the paperwork granting permission for Val and Giles to take the Auster to France for the D-Day celebrations as a private undertaking flew through the dusty corridors of government as if on wings. Similarly, the French authorities facilitated their paperwork once they were assured that there were no objections from their British opposite numbers. Permission was obtained weeks before TW348 was ready for her final inspections, test flying, and the grant of a Certificate of Airworthiness.

There was so much that remained to be done in the less than eleven months left before the celebrations of the twenty-fifth anniversary D-Day would be upon them.

The following evening, in the Smoke Room at the Old White Hart 'the Team' had meeting to progress their plans for getting to Normandy to join in the celebrations. There was still quite a lot to do before G-UNNR would be ready for the long flight across the English Channel. They pulled out the "to do" list that they had made so many months ago. Because the aircraft was effectively still a 'kit of parts,' albeit larger parts in the main, they realised that there was still quite a task ahead of them if they were going to be ready for the twenty-fifth anniversary celebrations marking the invasion of 'Fortress Europe' over the beaches of Normandy. They had made the major decisions regarding the cockpit fit out; civilian seats would be fitted, since neither were too comfortable with the thought of sitting on parachute packs. A modern VHF radio was on order, the original P2 compass would be refitted, and they would not fit a modern vacuum driven direction indicator to replace the original bezel reading instrument. They would keep the bulky artificial horizon which, due to the length of its case, had to be mounted centrally above the panel. Most of the wiring and the control cables had been run but could not be terminated until the assembly of the airframe, wings and empennage had been completed. Similarly, until the instrument panel and the flying controls were installed the cables to the rudder, elevators, trim tab, ailerons and flaps could not be made off. In order to be ready for the fitting of the instrument panel the fuel tank had to be set in place. They had been able to do the necessary restoration work to the firewall without having to remove it, although it had been stripped bare of the fittings that it carried.

Val had taken all the instruments and the two halves of the panel to Cranfield so that he could work on them when he was not preoccupied with his academic work. The Instrument Shop at Cranfield had done a great job overhauling, testing, and certificating the instruments and Val had fitted them after he had given the panel sections a thorough clean and re-paint in military olive-green drab. The ground-power master switch, magneto switches and light switches had been cleaned, tested and reinstated before the panel halves were carefully packed into wooden crates ready for transport back to Upham Manor where they were installed on the day following their delivery. The sub-panel, in which the engine controls were mounted, was fitted immediately before the instrument panel sections were bolted onto the cockpit frames. Giles had fabricated a tray into which their VHF radio was fitted, and this was mounted over the right-hand half of the instrument in front of the second Pilot's seat. The tray was set at a slight angle such that the Pilot-in-Command had a better view of the knobs, dials and the 'windows' in which the selected frequencies were displayed. With the panel complete and in place they were able to connect up the wiring to the various switches and install the vacuum pipework between the pair of venturi tubes, mounted on the port side of the fuselage forward of the Pilot's door, to the artificial horizon, the Reid and Sigrist Mk 1A turn and slip indicator, and the direction indicator.

The next task was to connect the engine instruments, oil pressure, cylinder head temperature, and tachometer. The electrical instruments, ammeter and voltmeter, and the 'starter motor engaged' lamp were more quickly coupled up. The trickiest wiring job was the installation of the individual 'transmit' or 'press-to-talk' buttons, which were mounted on the top of the dual control sticks. These 'PTT' switches were connected to a radio control box to ensure the radio transmitter would be activated, and the receiver supressed when making radio calls. Also, when either the P1 or P2 'PTT' was depressed the microphones on other Pilot's and passengers' headsets would be isolated.

The most demanding job now facing the team was the fitting of the undercarriage and the all-important bungee cord suspension system. The wheels were simply fitted to drum brake assemblies which in turn were mounted on a backplate which held the brake shoes, brake adjustment and spring release mechanism through which the stub-axle protruded. From the back of the undercarriage structure a steel tube strut was angled upward toward the centre of the fuselage; terminated in a plate which was designed to prevent the elasticated rubber suspension bungee cords from becoming detached. In the lower part of the fuselage a pair of substantial lugs were an integral part of the tubular fuselage structure between the Pilot and co-Pilot seats. The fitting of the bungee cords over these lugs was the cause of much sweating and swearing even with the use of the special tools that Teddy Neale had lent to them, once they sought his help following several unsuccessful attempts using tyre levers, the security of the undercarriage was completed by fitting safety wires that would prevent the undercarriage legs from splaying out in the unlikely event of the loss of a bungee cord.

The cockpit area was virtually complete: the P type compass remained to be mounted on its brackets on the floor between the seats, the safety harnesses had to be affixed to their anchor points on the structural tubes in the roof and at floor level. The cockpit glazing panels had to

be fitted to wooden frames which had been installed at the same time as the wooden formers and stringers had been fitted on the steel tube framework of the fuselage. The glazing panels were made of a strong acrylic plastic, all of these with the exception of the top panel were flat. The top panel, formed be a vacuum moulding process to produce a slightly domed shape, had been obtained from the Beagle-Rearsby factory where it had been held in the stores following the conversion of thirteen surplus to military requirements AOP Mark V models to civilian Mark V alpha variants in the late nineteen-fifties.

With the control sticks, rudder pedals, and heel operated brake pedals installed it was an easy task to connect and adjust the flying controls to the cables which had previously been run through the fuselage, and undercarriage fairings before the fabric coverings had been fitted. The aileron control wires had been installed in the wings but until the wings were fitted to the fuselage, they could not be connected to the control sticks. They had decided that the final fitting of the wings would have to be done at Shoreham under the supervision of Teddy Neale's riggers to satisfy the requirements that the build must be signed off by the Design Authority, the Auster Aeroplane Company, which of course was now incorporated within the Beagle Company. With the aeroplane essentially complete and assembled as far as was practicable thoughts turned to transporting it to Shoreham.

Giles came up with what seemed like a simple solution; he would clamp the tailwheel, which was free to castor, onto the floor of the Landrover close to the tailgate, the rear of the fuselage would be tied down with a rope over a sack stuffed with straw to prevent damage to the aircraft fabric. They were getting the material together to fit the clamp for the tailwheel when Jeannie asked, "where are you going to put the wings?" Giles and Valentine looked at each other, then at Jeannie before saying, in unison, "on the trailer of course." She smiled at them. "So why not put the airframe on the trailer as well and use one vehicle to take the whole caboodle to Shoreham? If there is a bit of an overhang at the back it won't matter, will it? Having everything on the big trailer, with weight of the engine well forward, it might be more stable on the tow than the aircraft running on its main undercarriage wheels with the weight at the back." Val looked miffed for a few seconds before bursting out laughing. "Trust my beautiful clever girl to make us look a right pair of clowns!" With everything loaded to Jeannie's satisfaction, G-UNNR was trailered off the be erected at the Beagle-Shoreham factory in readiness for its final inspections, the application of the camouflage and invasion stripe paint scheme, weighing and the all-important test flights to ensure that the aircraft was correctly rigged for safe, stable, flight within the specified design parameters.

Chapter 15

The call of the skies

G-UNNR was off loaded from the trailer onto the apron into the front of the principal hangar. It immediately drew a small crowd of interested workers, and others, who were wondering what was going on. Teddy Neale took charge and gave a quick rundown on why the aircraft was there, and what was to be done to prepare her for her return to the skies over Normandy for the duration of the celebrations associated with the Twenty-fifth anniversary of D-Day. He turned to Giles, Val, and Jeannie, "We'll take her from here, I afraid that I can't let you work in the hangar since you aren't employed by the firm and would not be covered by our employee insurance scheme. You can stand back and watch what we are doing but you will inevitably spend a lot of time just hanging about." With a grin he added. "Some it will be just watching paint dry."

Ted had allocated the work to an experienced team of riggers who set to work checking the wings and flying control surfaces for any damage in transit before setting them in place on trestles ready for fitting onto the fuselage. It had been decided that the aircraft would be painted in its wartime camouflage scheme once it had been erected and was ready to go for weighing. The tailplane and elevators were quickly mounted on the fuselage attachment points and, once their positions had been checked for symmetry the top and bottom stays were bolted in place before retaining bolts were tightened and wire-locked in place. Similarly, the rudder was fitted to the hinges on the stern post that formed the rear edge of the tailfin. The two-core electric cable that fed the taillight was pushed through into the fin and pulled down into the rear fuselage where it was terminated, connecting it to the wiring loom that had been installed by the team at Manor Farm. The elevator was mounted on the hinges on the trailing edges of the fixed tailplane structures and secured with locking wire. The flying controls operated by the rudder pedals, joystick, and the trimming handle were connected by thin steel cables, which were threaded through fairlead eyes to reduce friction and snagging on the airframe, to the rudder, elevator, and the moveable trim tab which was mounted in the trailing edge of the port elevator.

The wings were manoeuvred into place from the tall trestle stands and pushed onto the spigots designed to locate them on the upper tubes of the airframe over the cockpit. Whilst the wings were being mounted the electric cables to the dynamo, which was set into the leading edge of the starboard wing, and wingtip mounted navigation lights were pulled through into the cockpit together with the aileron cables that had been put in place before the fabric had been applied to the wing structures. Once the wings were correctly positioned the Vee shaped lift struts were bolted to lugs located on the lower sides of wing spars approximately two thirds of the way along the wing. The inboard ends were bolted to fuselage framework beneath the cockpit doors where the main undercarriage was also attached. The intermediate 'H' shaped jury struts set at the mid-point of the lift strut assemblies were set in place and the retaining bolts fitted and locked off. The copper pipe work connecting the pitot head, mounted on the port side jury strut assembly was connected to a flexible section of pipework at the root of the wing which was in turn connected to the airspeed indicator, altimeter and vertical speed indicator in the instrument panel. Once the wings were checked for symmetry, angle of attack, and dihedral the wing retaining bolts were tightened and wire locked. The aileron cables were adjusted, and the turnbuckles wire locked. The finishing touch of fitting the wing root cuffs which covered the wing attachment points, and smoothed the airflow at the wing roots, had the aircraft complete. She was then ready for transfer to the paint shop.

With all the cockpit glazing, pitot head, and other external fitments masked off, the painters set about laying on the base layer of the modern two-pack paint which worked well with the polyester ceconite fabric. The interior painting had all been completed by the restoration team at Manor Farm which looked very professionally finished. With the base coat hardened off and rubbed down the finishing coats of dark green and brown were applied in accordance with the standard pattern used in nineteen forty-four. The RAF roundels on the fuselage and the wings were carefully marked up. These, together with the aircraft serial number TW348 were hand painted in-situ by a signwriter. The black and white invasion recognition stripes were added as the final touch.

The engine had been run on the bench, and was bedded in, before it was mounted on the engine bearers. The fuel line and the air intake filter box were connected to the carburettor. The 'Ki-gas' primer line was connected to the inlet manifold. The exhaust manifold and the twin exhaust pipes were fitted before the connections were made to the instruments and the engine controls. Finally, the starter motor and magneto earthing connections, via switches on the instrument panel, together with other essential electrical connections in the engine bay were made off. The engine cowls were fitted and secured, before the newly cleaned and polished propeller was refitted onto its shaft. A plate, on which the Auster logo was embossed, was fitted over the hub of the propellor before the retaining bolts were inserted and torqued down. Once the propellor had been both statically and dynamically balanced the retaining bolts were re-torqued and wire locked.

Teddy Neale called Giles to tell him that she was ready to be moved from the paint shop to the flight test hanger later that day; he suggested that it would be a good time to come to Shoreham to see what they had done and to take photographs to record the event. Sadly, Valentine was tied up at Cranfield and could not get away to join the fun, Jane was of course invited. They drove over in Jane's Sunbeam arriving just as G-UNNR was about to be pushed out of the paint shop. She gleamed in the sunlight looking, as indeed she was, a perfect example of a factory finished machine. In fact, she was looking better that she had when she was issued to the RAF for service with 659 Air Observation Squadron in nineteen forty-four. Jane quickly got to work with the camera taking photographs from every angle possible and finishing her shoot with a group picture of the Beagle team: Giles and Teddy were standing either side of the engine cowling with the rest of the team lined up from wingtip to wingtip across the front of the aircraft. One of the airport fire crew took over the camera so that Jane could be included in a group photograph, and one of Giles and Jane together standing in front of the aircraft.

Teddy had called the Senior Works Test Pilot James Pearce, universally known in the business as Jimpee, over for a conference regarding the test flying programme and to work through the mountain of formal paperwork that had been generated during the restoration work. Jimpee took his time to ensure that there were no errors, and nothing had been missed. He checked all the Certificates of Conformity, the Worksheets and the signatures of the engineers who had either carried out or had supervised the work of others. He also checked that the second signatures of the Licenced Engineers responsible for checking the accuracy of the work, security of the wire locking of all critical items, as well as compliance with the relevant specifications and airworthiness directives had been undertaken correctly.

Once he had satisfied himself that the paperwork was all in order Jimpee turned his attention to the aircraft. His first task was to determine the basic empty weight of the machine, followed by the aircraft prepared for service weight. Critical measurements had to be taken in order to determine the position of the empty weight centre of mass relative to a specified reference point on the airframe. Further measurements allowed the calculation of a weight and balance envelope in which stable, controllable, and safe flight would be obtained. The aircraft design specification allowed for a maximum all up weight of 1900 pounds, and an empty weight of 1160 pounds. G-UNNR tipped the scales at 1162 pounds: the extra 2 pounds. being attributed the weight of the front seat cushions which had been installed in place of the crew using seat pack parachutes. That left 738 pounds available for fuel, oil, crew and payload which was acceptable for airworthiness purposes.

Before taking to the skies Jimpee carried out the necessary electrical services checks to prove that the navigation lights worked. He checked that the correct coloured lenses were fitted with a red on the port wingtip, a green on the starboard and that a clear lens was fitted in the lamp mounting on the trailing edge of rudder. Whilst not normally fitted on a civil aircraft the belly mounted military recognition lights were also checked for the correct lens colours and functionality. The cockpit interior was illuminated with a red light to preserve the crew's night vision. Landing and separate taxying lights mounted on the port lift struts were both lit, and the taxying lamp was focused onto the ground several feet to the front and the side of the aircraft. All switches were then returned to the 'off' position and the lights checked to ensure that they had been extinguished.

Jimpee then undertook a fingertip inspection of aircraft skin, flying control surfaces, bolts with wire locked nuts, and all the relevant fastenings for the inspection panels and engine cowlings. His inspection was completed to his satisfaction after he had given the wings, tailplane, and tailfin a vigorous shaking to prove that they were firmly affixed to the airframe. He completed his 'outside' checks with a flick of his wrist to spin the windmill blades that drove the dynamo that was housed in the starboard wing. He had meticulously placed a check mark against each item as he had made his inspection and was satisfied that nothing was amiss.

With the aircraft apparently airworthy his next task was to move it to the compass base, which was situated away from any possible sources of magnetic interference, where the 'P' type compass was to be calibrated, and to have the degrees of residual error at the principal points of the compass recorded on an error card attached to the compass bowl. The compass fitter took great care aligning the aircraft to each of the cardinal points in turn and making minute alterations to the compensating magnets built into the bowl of the instrument at each point. He then went on to repeat the exercise at the intermediate principal points before repeating the whole exercise with very fine adjustments until he was satisfied that the compass was set up to be as true as was practicable for each of the principal points. The aircraft was now ready to be taken aloft.

The engine oil level was checked to ensure that the sump had been correctly filled, the fuel tank had been filled to the maximum fifteen imperial gallons specified, Jimpee had recorded his weight as 160 pounds and he had the rear cockpit area loaded with ballast to bring the total weight up the maximum take-off weight of 1900 pounds He allowed a couple of pounds for fuel that would be burned whilst running up the engine for the power checks and taxying prior to take-off.

Jimpee had planned to make a short flight to get the feel of the control harmony, and to determine whether the fixed aileron and rudder trim tabs would need adjustment. The whole Manor Farm team, Jasper, Giles, Valentine, Jane, Jeannie, and Freddie were present to witness the first flight of G-UNNR. Jimpee climbed aboard, settled himself into the cushioned left hand, Captain's, seat and, after making sure that the safety harnesses for the second Pilot and rear passenger seats were secured, he gave the four-point harness for his seat a strong tug to satisfy himself that it was properly secured to the main airframe tubes before strapping himself in.

A visual check of the instrument panel and controls was next on his checklist:

1. All switches and lights off,

2. Instrument glasses free from cracks, dirt, and instrument dials clearly visible.

3. Instruments displaying the expected readings,

4. With the altimeter set to zero the pressure setting was showing the airfield pressure (QFE,)

5. Change the altimeter pressure setting to the regional mean sea level pressure (QNH). *{At Shoreham the airfield elevation is 7 feet above the mean sea level, the QFE and QNH are separated by 0.23 millibar which is too small a difference to be determined on an altimeter.}*

6. Check flying controls, including the elevator trimmer, for full and free movement whilst observing the respective control surfaces react to the control inputs in the correct sense.

7. Check flap operation, ensuring that the flap control lever fully engages with the appropriate detent for each setting – Take-off, intermediate, and full. Observe the travel of the split flap surfaces and check for symmetry of operation. Return the flap lever to retracted and check engagement with the 'raised' detent, and that the flaps have symmetrically seated back into the trailing edge of the wings.

8. Check the operation of the handbrake, fully apply the brakes using the heel operated pedals, pull out the handbrake lever to the furthest extent possible and release the heel brake pedals. Check that the detents hold the hand operated brake lever in place. Release the brake lever and check that it has moved to the fully released position. Set the brakes 'on.'

9. Check that the doors are properly closed and latched shut, Open the sliding 'windows' in each door, close and reopen the windows. Check the window locking screws hold the moveable panes in place.

10. Operate the throttle and mixture plungers fully forward and return to fully extended out of the panel. Apply the control lock to the throttle, check that the plunger cannot be moved.

11. Operate the fuel shut off cock from closed to open and closed again. Ensuring that there was no undue stiffness, or slackness, whilst it was being moved.

Jimpee both read out each item on his checklist and verbally confirmed that the actions were completed to his satisfaction before ticking the check box against each one. He was now ready to check that the radio was working, he would use it to request permission to start the engine and perform the engine checks. Without reference to a printed check list, he flipped the master switch on and paused to check for any signs of an electrical short circuit. "Good," he said to himself, "no hot insulation smells or smoke in the cockpit."

He switched on the radio and confirmed that it was correctly tuned to the 'Shoreham Tower' frequency. Before attempting to make any transmissions he visually scanned the aerodrome circuit for any traffic that might be about to call the Controller in the tower: the circuit was clear, and nothing was heard from other Pilots in the local area. He adjusted the volume and squelch controls in order to remove any static noise in his headphones, then depressing the 'PTT' switch in the top of the control column he spoke clearly, "Shoreham Tower, Golf Uniform November November Romeo radio check." He received an instant response, "Golf Uniform November November Romeo Shoreham Tower reading you strength five." Jimpee having heard the response very clearly shot back "five also, request engine start." The Controller again responded, this time shortening the call sign, with "Golf November Romeo start approved, call when ready to taxy." Jimpee called back "Golf November Romeo engine testing only at the moment, out." With that he switched off the radio to protect its components against damage from any current surge, or voltage spikes that might occur during engine start up. He ticked off radio checks complete on his check list.

He took a good look around his aircraft to make sure that, as far as he could see, there was nothing in the immediate vicinity that could be affected by the propwash when the engine started. He put his arm out of the Pilot's side window, which he had deliberately left open earlier, and signalled to the fireman standing by with a fire extinguisher ready to douse any engine fire that might break out on starting up. With his right hand he first selected 'fuel on,' then unscrewed the 'ki-gas' plunger allowing him to administer four forceful pumps, which sent neat fuel into the intake manifold, before resecuring it. He set the throttle approximately a quarter of an inch open and set the friction control to lightly hold it in place, the mixture control plunger was pushed fully home into the panel to the 'full rich' setting. He had been holding his left hand out with the thumb down, at this stage of the starting procedure he reversed his hand to give a thumbs up to the fireman. He withdrew his hand and flipped the magneto switches to 'on.' Whilst so doing he visually checked that the handbrake lever was set 'on' and placed his heels firmly onto the brake pedals. He called out "mags on" and holding the stick fully back with his left hand called out "clear prop." He again checked that there was no sign of anyone under the nose of the aircraft, he looked to the fireman who gave him a 'thumbs up' and satisfied that it was safe to so do he called "contact" and pressed the starter button which was located on the right-hand half of the instrument panel. The 'starter engaged' warning light illuminated as the starter motor turned the engine, one…. two…. three blades, the engine coughed without backfiring, four… five… blades, the engine coughed again and then caught with all four cylinders firing smoothly. Releasing the starter motor button, he checked that 'starter engaged' light had gone out, it had. The fireman appeared satisfied that there was no fire in the engine intake or under the cowling: he waved to Jimpee and called "all good boss," before he moved away to the side of the apron to watch the next stage of the testing process. Back to the check list, "engine start procedure OK" Jimpee said to himself as he ticked the boxes on his sheet.

The tachometer indicated a fast idle speed of 850 revolutions per minute. The oil pressure was starting to respond, rising slowly into the green banded arc on the gauge of 60 - 90 psi. After a few minutes the needle was showing a steady 75 psi. the cylinder head and oil temperatures had also settled in the centre of their respective permitted ranges. The figures were duly noted on the checklist. With the temperatures and pressures indicating 'in the green' the next task was to check the static performance of the engine: looking around once more to satisfy himself that the area was clear Jimpee gradually pushed the throttle plunger forward against the grip of the friction screw increasing the 'revs' and the power output of the engine. When the throttle plunger was fully forward the aircraft was starting to inch forward against the holding power of the brakes; Jimpee read 2150 rpm off the tachometer and reduced the power until the brakes once again appeared to be holding. He pulled the throttle plunger back a little further until the tachometer was reading a steady 1800 rpm. He noted maximum static rpm on his checklist and ticked the item as satisfactory. Again, he checked that the oil temperature and pressure readings were 'in the green' and that the cylinder head temperature was within limits, he placed three more tick marks on the checklist"All good so far" he said, "now let's see how magnetos are doing." With that he moved the left-hand magneto switch down into the 'off' position; the engine 'revs' dropped slightly by 90 rpm, moving the switch back to 'on' the 'revs' immediately increased back to the 1800 rpm that he had set earlier. He carried out the same test for the right-hand magneto. When he flipped the switch to 'off' the 'revs' dropped to 1700 rpm this time, and when he flipped the switch back to 'on' the tachometer showed 1800 rpm as before. "That's OK then" said Jimpee as he wrote 90L, 100R, diff 10 on his sheet. He operated the air intake heat control plunger to allow hot air from around the exhaust manifold to be fed into the carburettor: a drop of 150 rpm was immediately registered on the tachometer. He reset the air intake control to 'cold' and as before the engine rpm rose back to the steady 1800 rpm for which the throttle had been set. He repeated the magneto and 'hot air checks three times diligently recording the figures obtained. Satisfied with the figures obtained he pulled the throttle plunger fully back and recorded the resulting slow idle engine speed of 600 rpm "very good" he said to himself as he returned the throttle to the ground idle setting of 700 rpm. After a few seconds to let the engine settle into a steady idle he reset the power to give 1800 rpm on the tachometer and then slowly pulled the mixture control plunger back until the engine started to 'run rough' with a marked reduction in 'revs': he immediately pushed the mixture control back to 'full rich' then repeated the exercise a couple more times. Satisfied that the mixture control was performing as expected he again throttled back to the ground idle setting. He had one more check to complete, would the engine stop? He pulled the mixture control smoothly back through the range of weak mixture to the 'idle cut-off' position; the engine faltered and died with the propellor flicking through a few blades before ceasing to rotate. "Mags off, fuel off, master off" he said to himself before busying himself with his checklist notes. He released his seat harness, checking that the hand brake was still fully applied, he released the door and swung himself out of the cockpit. He called the fireman over, before releasing the fasteners on the engine cowlings and swinging them up to prop them open so that he could carry out a visual examination of the engine bay looking for signs of fuel, oil and exhaust gas leaks. There was no trace of any fire having started and extinguished: everything was spotlessly clean. 'No visible leaks' was duly noted on the engine test checklist sheets. He had noted the tendency to creep forward against the brakes when full power had been applied but he added in the remarks 'brake test satisfactory at this stage.'

Jimpee took the opportunity to take a personal needs break and have a few words with the Manor Farm group before going back to the task of clearing the aeroplane for the issue of the all-important Private Category Certificate of Airworthiness. He placed a new wad of forms on his clip board. These forms were pre-printed with fields in which he would record the important performance details of the aircraft during the flight. One page was devoted to the climb performance, over a five-minute period, which required highly accurate reading and recording of data every thirty seconds. At one-minute intervals additional data had to be gathered and recorded. It was important to record the outside air temperature and airspeed so that small corrections could be made to the indicated airspeed to compensate for the changes in air density as the climb progressed. An outside air temperature gauge was not a standard fitting for the AOP Mark V but Jimpee had insisted that one be mounted in the cockpit 'brow' glazing close to the port wing root. Test flying of this sort called for very high degrees of skill in handling the aircraft being flown and the ability to concentrate on several different tasks for minutes at a time.

As he returned to G-UNNR he called to Valentine, and the others who were there to witness the test flight, "all looks good so far. If she gets off the ground safely, I should be back in about forty-five minutes, anything less you will know that there's something not quite right." With that, and a cheery wave, he climbed into the cockpit. He quickly ran through the engine start checklist and called the Aerodrome Controller for permission to start the engine for a test flight in the local area. Once the engine was idling smoothly with the temperatures and pressures showing 'in the green' he recorded the engine data. Speaking to himself he recited his pre-taxy checks, "controls full and free movement, flying control surfaces moving in harmony with the controls. Trimmer fully aft, fully forward, trim tab moving in the correct sense, set neutral. Flaps fully lowered, raised to intermediate and then to the take-off setting in the first detent, both sides operating symmetrically and to the necessary deflections with each setting of the flap lever. Harnesses secured, Pilot harness tightened and secure. Throttle friction set, mixture rich, carburettor heat selected 'off,' ki-gas primer in and locked. Visual check all round the apron, all clear, radio for taxy clearance." Whilst undertaking his checks Jimpee had been listening to the radio which was tuned to the 'tower' frequency, he made his call, "Golf Uniform November November Romeo operating as Tango Whiskey Tree Fower Ate request airfield information ." The Controller in the tower responded

"Tree Fower Ate active runway two wun, QFE wun zero wun tree millibars, regional QNH wun zero wun wun millibars, wind two hundred at ten knots. Cleared taxy holding point delta for two wun, report ready for departure." Jimpee responded "runway two wun, QFE won zero wun tree, Regional QNH wun zero wun wun, taxy Delta, tree fower ate." He applied the heel brakes, released the handbrake, and gently advanced the throttle. Once he was satisfied that the heel brakes were effective he released them and the aircraft rolled forward. A little burst of power was required to move, one wheel at a time, off the concrete apron and onto the grass taxiway. Full right rudder and a small burst of power produced the desired effect of swinging the nose of the aircraft to the right and once aligned with the taxiway a sharp tap on the left rudder pedal and a reduction of power had the aircraft running smoothly in a straight line to cross the end of runway three two; then turning left following the taxiway to cross the threshold for runway two eight before reaching holding point Delta for Runway two one.

In common with nearly all aircraft with tailwheel undercarriage the view over and to the right of the nose was severely restricted since the aircraft's nose was higher than the Pilot's eyeline. Jimpee was forced to follow a gentle zig-zag path along the taxiway to the holding point to ensure that he had a clear view ahead by looking, alternately, along either side of the nose. Upon reaching the holding point he swung the aircraft into wind, the power was reduced to idle, the heel brakes were applied and held on until the handbrake had been set.

Pre-take-off checks were the next step; Jimpee again vocalized the list of actions that were ingrained in his memory. "Into wind, brakes on, clear all around, full and free movement of the control stick, rudder pedals checked whilst taxying, stick fully aft and with mixture rich advance the throttle: check the brakes holding, throttle fully open and brakes holding ….. hummn - only just, she's starting to creep forward, check maximum static revs … 2150 rpm noted on knee pad, temperatures and pressures all good, reduce throttle to 1800 rpm and check magnetos …. Left 'off' revs drop 100 rpm and noted, left 'on' … 1800 rpm restored, right mag' 'off' revs drop 100 rpm and restored to 1800 rpm when switched back 'on,' noted no differential drop between the magnetos when switched 'off.' Carburettor heat set to 'hot' and the engine revs dropped by 150 rpm, returning the carburettor heat to 'cold' restored the engine revs to 1800 rpm. Throttle retarded to full idle, note 650 rpm and the engine running smoothly. Good to go. Final cockpit check: trimmer neutral, rear seat harness secured, passenger door closed and secure, passenger side harness is secure, ammeter reading slight discharge but the dynamo isn't being driven fast enough yet, radio 'on,' and tower frequency selected – check squelch and volume controls, cockpit light, navigation light, taxy and landing light switches 'off', oil temperature and pressure gauges ok, cylinder head temperature ok, fuel gauge showing full fifteen gallons, flight instruments glasses intact and reading correctly with altimeter pressure sub-scale set 1013 millibars altimeter reading zero, synchronise the direction indicator with the compass to show 200 degree magnetic, master switch is 'on,' outside air temperature is plus fifteen degrees Celsius – note on the test data sheet, Pilot side door is closed and secure, flap lever set for take-off … one notch and secure, Pilot harness fitted correctly and tightened, fuel cock set to 'on' and no belly tank fitted, DI set and reading 200 degrees, carburettor heat control fully forward –'off', mixture fully forward – 'rich', throttle friction finger tight, 'Ki-gas' primer in and locked, all OK." With that he pressed the PTT switch on the top of the control stick and called the Controller in the tower: "tree fower ate, ready for take-off runway two wun." The immediate response was "tree fower ate, cleared take-off runway two wun wind two hundred at niner knots." Jimpee read back his clearance "cleared take-off runway two wun, tree fower ate."

With that clearance he released the handbrake, advanced the throttle and taxied forward to align the aircraft with the centre line of the grass runway, satisfying himself that the fully castoring tailwheel was straight he centred the control stick. After a final check to assure himself that the DI was showing 210 degrees magnetic, he smoothly applied full power.

As the propellor spun faster the combined effects of the airflow spiralling clockwise round the fuselage and the unbalanced aerodynamic forces generated by the propellor whilst in a tail down attitude would have caused the tail to swing away to the right, pushing the aircraft's nose to the left. Even before the effect of those combined forces were felt Jimpee pressed the right rudder pedal to counteract the tendency of the aircraft to swing away from the centre line of the runway. With increasing airspeed, the elevators became more effective lifting the tailwheel off the ground to bring the aircraft into a level attitude. The gyroscopic force generated by the change of attitude on the propellor disc further increased the tendency of the aircraft to swing to the left. Jimpee instinctively increased the pressure on the right rudder pedal thereby maintaining an arrow straight track along the runway before gently, but firmly, easing the control stick back to lift the aircraft away from the runway into the ground effect. He allowed the airspeed increase before increasing the back pressure on the stick and establishing the aircraft into a climb.

The first part of the test flight was to climb away from the runway at the best angle of climb airspeed, called Vx, which was given in the

Pilot operating notes as forty miles per hour, and note the time taken to climb to fifty feet above the ground. Thereafter, the climb was to be carried out at the best rate of climb airspeed, Vy , to attain level flight at five hundred feet above the mean sea level. The altimeter subscale was adjusted to show 1010 millibars and the aircraft was levelled off at exactly five hundred feet on that pressure setting. Jimpee reduced the power and adjusted the attitude of the aircraft to maintain an indicated airspeed of one hundred miles per hour. He then moved the trimmer control until there was no pressure on the stick with the aircraft flying straight and level.

He checked the turn and slip indicator and the direction indicator, the indicators showed that the aircraft was in a gentle turn to port and the left wing was starting to go down banking the aircraft in that direction. He applied a gentle pressure to the right rudder pedal which stopped the angle of bank from increasing, further pressure on that pedal caused the bank angle to decrease and the yaw to the left was stopped. Once the wings level attitude was regained he slightly reduced the pressure from his right foot and applied an almost imperceptible pressure on the control stick to maintain straight and level flight. He made a note to the effect that the rudder trim tab required adjustment. He was satisfied that the ailerons were perfectly set and that with the stick marginally off-centre the aircraft maintained straight and level flight, albeit with slight right rudder applied. He decided that the rudder trim adjustment would be minor and that there was nothing to be gained by returning to Shoreham rather than continuing with his test flight. It was now time to make the long five-minute climb maintaining the best rate airspeed compensating for the decrease in temperature with increasing altitude. The timed climb was completed without any issues at an altitude of three thousand three hundred and seventy feet. The next manoeuvres were designed to determine the stall, spin, and spin recovery characteristics of the aircraft so he continued to climb until he reached his safety altitude of five thousand feet. Whilst maintaining the trimmed airspeed he levelled out in preparation for the stalling and spinning trials.

He first checked his location to ensure that he was not over a built-up area and positively identified his position as approximately one mile inland and five miles west of Shoreham. He carried out a series of 'S' turns to the right and left using bank angles of thirty and sixty degrees allowing him both to gain a better feel for the handling characteristics of the aircraft and to ensure that there were no other aircraft nearby. Satisfied that he had the sky to himself, and that the engine instruments were indicating that all was as it should be, he headed towards the coast. After pulling the carburettor heat control fully 'on' he gradually retarded the throttle whilst easing back on the stick, thereby maintaining altitude and reducing the airspeed by one mile per hour per second. As the airspeed indicator needle dropped towards thirty-five miles per hour the controls started to feel 'sloppy,' less responsive, and as the needle touched the thirty-three miles per hour mark Jimpee felt a soft buffet on the stick from the elevators. There was a little shudder through the airframe, and he saw the left wingtip dropping slowly towards the horizon. He smartly touched the right rudder pedal to prevent the aircraft from yawing off to the left, simultaneously he relaxed the back pressure on the control stick and smoothly applied full power. The carburettor heat control plunger was swiftly returned to the 'off' position. He noted that the 'clean' unaccelerated stall had occurred at thirty-three miles per hour with slight buffet and port wing drop. Straight and level flight was recovered with no loss of altitude. He repeated the exercise and obtained the same results; satisfied the aircraft was quite benign in the simple stall he set the flaps to landing configuration and repeated the stalling exercise. This time the airspeed indicator was showing thirty miles per hour before he felt the buffet effect and at twenty-eight miles per hour the left wing dropped rather more sharply than previously. A swift 'boot-full' of right rudder was administered, to prevent the aircraft from both rolling and yawing to the left, whilst completing the standard stall recovery actions as before. He noted that the aircraft had lost nearly one hundred feet of altitude during the manoeuvre.

He was now ready to investigate the spin and spin recovery characteristics, another series of clearing turns and returning to the five-thousand-foot safety altitude he altered his heading to proceed eastwards approximately two miles out to sea, parallel with the coastline, towards Shoreham. "No putting off the inevitable I suppose" said Jimpee to himself. Spinning an aeroplane isn't exactly one of the most pleasant of manoeuvres since the aircraft is stalled, yawing, pitching, and rolling all at the same time. Just as he had done for the stalling tests he applied carburettor heat and retarded the throttle gently, reducing the airspeed as before whilst maintaining altitude. This time he didn't fully close the throttle but left it set at 1300 rpm whilst continuing to raise the nose of the aircraft. The airspeed indicator needle was starting flicker around the twenty-five mile per hour mark when Jimpee pressed the left rudder pedal firmly forward as far as possible: the aircraft shuddered, and the nose of aircraft reared skyward at the same time the left wing dropped suddenly below the horizon dragging the aircraft inverted then continuing the roll into a steep nose down attitude. The aircraft was spinning, the ground below appeared to be going round like a vinyl record on turntable. Jimpee counted the number of times the coastline at Shoreham passed by the nose of the aircraft "one, two, three, four, five, no sign of the spin becoming flat, very well let's recover." With that he fully closed the throttle, released the back pressure and moved the stick fully forward whilst simultaneously applying full right rudder. After approximately half a rotation the spinning motion stopped. The aircraft was in steep nose down attitude with the wings levelled against the horizon. He held the rudder slightly right of neutral as the aircraft continued diving and the airspeed increased. Jimpee noted that the altimeter was 'unwinding' through two thousand seven-hundred feet. He selected the carburettor heat 'off' and smoothly opened the throttle whilst gently pulling back on the stick in order to establish a climb back to his safety altitude. He repeated the exercise, but this time he applied full right rudder as the aircraft stalled: the left wing had started to drop, it checked and then the aircraft quickly snapped over into a right-handed spin. Jimpee initiated the standard spin recovery actions after five full rotations being satisfied again that there had been no tendency for the spin to flatten. This time instead of recovering into a climb he maintained forward pressure on the control stick, the speed quickly built up in the dive until with the design limit 'never exceed speed', Vne, of one hundred and fifty miles per hour was showing on the airspeed indicator he gently eased back on the control stick to avoid entering a 'high G' stall. He levelled out at one thousand feet above the mean sea level. A quick instrument check and a visual examination of the airframe as far as was possible had him satisfied that the aircraft was fit for service. He carried out a couple of 'clearing turns' to establish that he had not inadvertently flown into the path of another aircraft before setting his course back to Shoreham.

He returned to Shoreham after making a radio call to announce his impending arrival. The Controller advised "Tree fower ate, join for runway two wun QFE wun zero wun tree millibars." He repeated the essential details of his clearance, "runway two wun, wun zero wun tree millibars, tree fower ate." He flew a curving approach, as he did so he slowed the aircraft to fifty miles per hour, worked the trimmer until he felt no pressure on the stick, and then set two stages of flap as he started his turn onto the final approach path. He fully lowered the flaps as he passed through 300 feet and lined up with the runway. He slowly closed the throttle whilst smoothly and deliberately pulling the control stick back into his stomach. The aircraft touched down on all three wheels simultaneously just as the control stick reached the rear stops. With his feet dancing lightly on the rudder pedals he held the aircraft to the centre line of the runway until she was almost stationary. A quick burst of power had her moving off the runway and taxying back to the apron where Valentine and Giles were anxiously waiting. Jimpee applied a short burst of power, kicked the left rudder, and swung the nose of the aircraft into the wind before shutting down the engine, completing his post flight cockpit checks, and making his final notes on his test sheets.

Valentine and Giles ran over to him calling out "well?" Jimpee grinned at them as he climbed out of the cockpit, "she'll do, just needs a tweak on the rudder trim tab. Once that's done I'll take her up again to be certain that the riggers have set it correctly and then we are all done and dusted" he said somewhat laconically. Then with a broad smile he continued, "in fact she's as nice a lady as I've the pleasure of testing. You've done a brilliant job: a fine tribute to your dad Val. I'm looking forward to seeing her being displayed at Auster Pilot Club events and other places. Now I'm sorry to say that I have to go into the office to fully write up the test flight and prepare the C of A paperwork before we can do anything else."

They thanked Jimpee for his efforts and all the help that he had given them before inviting him to join them later in the beautiful Art Deco terminal building's restaurant where they were to meet up with Jane and Jeannie who had, quite sensibly, gone off to find a comfortable place to wait and watch the aircraft movements on the airfield when Jimpee departed to conduct the test flight. The ladies had enjoyed a pot of tea and cream cakes whilst they chatted about Alex, his aeroplane and its restoration. They spoke about Val and Jeannie's relationship with him which turned the conversation to the subject of marriage and their future lives together even though Val hadn't made a proposal of marriage. Jane said "if I know my son, he will be rather shy about it; but I do know that he has strong feelings and cares deeply about you. He will get around to asking you to marry him before long, and when he does, we need to be ready for him with plans for your wedding: not that I am trying to rush you but between us we will have to steer him into what will be the best for everyone in the end." That conversation was quickly ended when they spotted Valetine and Giles making their way across the restaurant towards their table.

Jane smiled sweetly and Jeannie tried to look innocent as Jane asked them if they wanted to have tea and cakes, "we are celebrating, aren't we?" she asked, although she knew the good news they bore from the grins on their faces and their jaunty step as they had approached the table. "Yes, we certainly are celebrating. Jimpee is satisfied with the aircraft, we have to make a small adjustment to the fixed rudder trim tab, but he is at this very minute completing the paperwork for submission to the Registration Board, he said that he will speak to the local Inspector to ensure that there are no delays in getting the

Certificate of Airworthiness issued. He said that we will have to let him have cheque to go with the documentation before we leave today." Giles said "we still can't fly her ourselves, so we will have keep the champagne on ice until we have all the aircraft documents signed sealed and delivered, but that won't take very long." Good to his word Jimpee eventually came into the restaurant to join them. He asked Jane if she had the cheque made out to the Air Registration Board as the fee for the C of A. She opened her handbag and dug out a receipt for the fee that she had paid when she had first applied for the aircraft registration and the issue of a Certificate of Airworthiness "I'm ahead of the game Jimpee," she said with an impish grin. "Thank you for all you and the team here at Shoreham have done for us, you have no idea just how much it means to us and especially to me to have Alex's aeroplane fully restored and to such a high standard. Now, how about a cup of tea and a nice cream cake as a reward?" They sat and chatted about their hopes for the future and especially about the planned trip to Normandy for the Twenty-fifth anniversary of the D-Day landings. Jimpee gave Val and Giles some useful titbits of information regarding getting the best performance out of their aircraft and the best figures to use when flight planning so as to ensure that they had a 'bit left in the tank' at the end of every flight.

A celebration to mark the return of Captain Alex Shooter's Auster TW348, officially known as G-UNNR, was planned for the following weekend. All the necessary paperwork had been issued and placed in a document wallet which was entrusted to Giles as the official owner of the aircraft: he and Valentine had been sent off to Shoreham to collect the star attraction of the day. Everyone who had been involved in the rescue and restoration of Alex Shooter's aeroplane had been invited to the party at the Manor Farm hanger. Jane and Jeannie had the preparations for receiving Alex's aeroplane back at the former RAF Manor Farm well in hand. Valentine and Giles had an emotional send off from the Beagle factory at Shoreham and it was with tears of gratitude in his eyes that Valentine climbed into the cockpit to prepare for the relatively short flight home with Jimpee by his side in the right-hand seat. Valentine had insisted that Jimpee accompany him. He said it was only fitting that Jimpee as the Factory Test Pilot should be an honoured guest at the party, he was as much a star as the aircraft. Val also admitted to Jimpee that because it was such an emotional experience that he felt he needed the support of a steadying Copilot to ensure that there would be no drama associated with the flight. With the latter reason foremost in his mind Valentine suggested that rather than fly directly to Manor Farm they should fly a series of exercises to allow him to become comfortable with the handling of the Auster Mark V, which differed in certain respects from the aerobatic Aiglet models on which he had gained his Pilot's Licence. The Aiglet trainers had shorter wings which, together with a slightly heavier and more powerful engine, gave a higher wing loading than that of the Mark V which made the stall, spin, and landing characteristics slightly different.

Valentine carefully, and thoroughly, went through the pre-flight checks even though he knew that the aircraft had not been touched since being finally cleared after the rudder trim had been adjusted to Jimpee's satisfaction less than a week ago. The factory ground handlers had made sure that the fuel tank was full, and the control locks had been removed from the flying control surfaces: nevertheless, Val checked that the control locks were securely stowed along with the wheel chocks before he had settled himself into the Captain's seat. With a 'thumbs up' to the ground crew, and a call of "clear prop" he started the engine and sat back letting it warm up whilst checking that the starter motor warning light had extinguished, and both the oil temperature and pressures gauges were starting to respond with the needles moving toward the green arcs on the dials. When he was satisfied that all was good, he turned to Jimpee and said, "I'm so excited to be doing this, just think we are going to fly my dad's 'plane." Jimpee smiled at him and said "yes, it's quite a moment. Would you like me to make the radio calls, it would make me feel like part of the team." He replied with a catch in his voice, "Yes please, good idea, I'm feeling a bit emotional still and not sure that I could manage to speak any too clearly right now."

Once cleared to the holding point for runway two one Valentine released the handbrake and applied a trickle of power. TW348 rolled forward and as Val increased the power a little more to move the aircraft at a brisk walking pace he kicked the rudder pedals right and left to clear his view ahead. He gave the ground crew a wave as he taxied away from the apron. Power checks and a final 'full and free' check of the controls complete Val looked across to Jimpee and said, "time to go." They got their take-off clearance and Val taxied forward onto the runway making sure that the aircraft was tracking straight along the centre line. Jimpee called to Val, "right rudder," as the nose started to swing left when Val applied full power, "remember this is an American Lycoming engine and the prop is driven clockwise rather than in the anticlockwise direction of the de Haviland Gypsy engines that you are used to." Val concentrated on the task of keeping straight as the Auster gathered speed. The elevators became responsive to the increasing airflow and the tail started to rise bringing the aircraft into a level attitude; Val instinctively counteracted the tendency of the aircraft to swung to the left and maintained a straight track along the centreline. A quick check of the instruments showed that the airspeed indicator was working. The needle was already past the marked 'clean' stalling speed. With a little more back pressure on the stick he had G-UNNR skipping over the grass, and then airborne. Valentine let out a great whoop of joy as the ground fell away beneath his wings.

His thoughts went immediately to his dad, he felt a connection with the man who had died before he was born and knew instantly that he had been cloaked in the mantle of Alexander James Shooter. The sensation of flying the Auster Mark V was electrifying, his senses were heightened, he felt completely at one with the machine and he knew that he was totally the master of the aircraft. He was speechless and sensed that he was detached from the world around him: but extremely situationally aware in respect of flying his aircraft. He became aware of Jimpee speaking with an edge of concern in his voice, "Val, Val, are you OK? Come on snap out of it we are off course and heading towards France!" Val was jerked out of the reverie, the detached sensation lifted, and he was aware that they were indeed heading away from the coast which was a mile or so behind them. Jimpee spoke again "are you OK lad? You seemed to go into a daze although it was obvious that you were in complete control of the aeroplane." Valentine looked across to his friend, smiled and said "Yes Jimpee I was miles and years away. I was with my dad and I'm not sure which of us was flying the 'plane. However, thanks to you I definitely have control now. Let's do a few turns, then a couple of stalls, and follow that with a practice approach to a precautionary landing before we set heading for Upham Manor. Val flew the exercises with an easy precision that he had never before been able to achieve. He revelled in the joy of pure flight and the ease with which the Auster responded to the control inputs, which seemed to be driven by his thoughts and unconscious movements.

All too soon they had Upham in sight, and smoke from the chimneys in the village indicated that there was a stiffish breeze blowing from sightly west of south. Val mentally plotted his approach to the north to south runway, he opted for a standard overhead join at one thousand five hundred feet on the regional QNH. As he crossed the middle of the former RAF aerodrome he reset the altimeter subscale to read height above the runway threshold. The altimeter showed one thousand one hundred and seventy feet. He swung the aircraft round in a gently descending left hand turn that placed him on the downwind leg of the circuit at exactly one thousand feet above the ground, he trimmed the aircraft to maintain level flight at fifty miles per hour and when he was abeam the threshold, he pulled the flap lever out of the 'up' detent and smoothly lowered the flaps to the approach setting. He selected 'hot' with the carburettor heat control and adjusted the throttle to maintain fifty miles per hour indicated on the airspeed indicator. The nose of the aircraft dropped to just below the horizon, providing Valentine with a clear view directly ahead. He juggled the stick to maintain his trimmed initial approach speed, and started the base leg turn as his height slowly decreased. He kept the threshold in his view such that as the turn progressed, and the aircraft descended, he didn't need to move his head or eyes to maintain a constant aspect approach. He started to roll out of the descending turn shortly before the extended centre line of the runway was reached. He selected carburettor heat 'off' and reached up with his left hand to release the flap lever detent then pulled the lever down firmly to set full flap. This increased the aerodynamic drag, increased the lift, and further lowered the nose of the aircraft, he quite subconsciously adjusted the power to compensate for the changes and with a little back pressure on the stick he slowed the aircraft until the airspeed indicator showed his chosen threshold speed of forty miles per hour. He quickly reached up with his right hand to operate the trimmer control removing the stick pressure on his left hand and thus maintained his threshold speed.

The aircraft swept over the boundary fence, then skimming a foot or so above the grass runway in the ground effect Valentine slowly and deliberately pulled the sick fully back whilst smoothly fully closing the throttle. G-UNNR slowed and as the nose came up into the three-point attitude she touched down like a feather perfectly in the centre of the runway. She skipped lightly due to the slight unevenness of the ground. Without really being aware of it Val was working the rudder pedals left and right to keep the aircraft rolling in a straight line as she slowed to a stop. A touch of power and a flick on the left rudder pedal had the Auster taxying across the grass towards her gaily decorated hanger. A large banner was draped across the doors: it read 'Welcome Home TW348.' Val carefully made the transition from the grass to the concrete apron in front of the hanger one wheel at a time. Then swinging her into the wind he shut down the engine with a flourish, applying full power and retarding the mixture control to the 'idle cut off' position before switching off the magnetos, fuel cock and the master switch. He set the brakes, released his harness, and jumped out of the cockpit into Jeannie's open arms and taking in her adoring look he pulled her to him and kissed her. "That has just made my day perfect" he said to her. "I'm not sure which I love the most, flying 348 or holding you close." Jeannie pulled a face at him, laughed, and said "the latter I hope!"

They walked arm in arm over to the hanger to open the doors. As they parted the doors they were greeted by a cheering mob of well-wishers and the whole team that had worked on the restoration project including, much to Valentine's surprise, Sir Henry Milner and the principal members of the Beagle factory team who had been instrumental in getting G-UNNR back into the air. Giles had driven like a maniac from Shoreham in order to be back in time for the arrival of the Auster. He pulled up on the apron just as Valentine parked TW348 in front of the hanger doors. He was just as astonished as Valentine when the party goers surged out with shouts of approval to view the star attraction. The party was underway with gusto and continued with speeches, stories of former times and memories, both good and poignant, together with toasts to all and sundry until the bar was all but run dry late in the evening.

During the course of the evening Valentine's Uncle Ollie drew him aside for a personal chat. Ollie had been in conversation with Jimpee sometime earlier during which Valentine's rather strangely detached and dreamlike state, as Jimpee had described it, had been mentioned. Ollie was concerned and with all the directness of a Senior Army Officer addressed his concerns head on. "I gather that shortly after take-off from Shoreham you appeared to Mr Pearce to have gone off into a world of your own. It was a good job that he was with you and managed to bring you back to reality. What was going on eh?" Valentine looked around before answering his uncle and being sure that nobody would overhear their conversation he said, "quite simply, uncle, I connected with my dad. I can't put it into words: but I seemed to be outside myself and dad was flying the Auster. I could sense his emotions and his thoughts regarding flying into action once he reached his Advanced Landing Ground in France. It wasn't at all scary, I felt completely calm and at ease as I got to know him as a person. Looking back now at the experience it could be considered a bit spooky, but it wasn't like that: it was special and very emotional. When we started flying my familiarisation exercises, I felt as though he was guiding me through them. Make no mistake I was fully focussed on the tasks in hand, but I was being talked through them by the best Instructor with whom I have ever flown." Ollie stood reflecting for a minute or so on what he had just been told. He then said gently, "my boy; that is really something for you to treasure. Your dad was a very special man and one of the most competent Pilots I have ever known. Furthermore, I know that he was an exceptional Instructor, his RAF and USAAF records bear witness of that. You have a great deal to live up to. Don't try too hard to be better than you need be, he will take care of you, and you will be a wonderful example of the man he was." With that Ollie squared his shoulders and reverting to his military persona declared, "now let's get these glasses refilled and drink to his memory, eh, what?"

Over the course of the next few weeks and months Valentine and Giles ranged far and wide in TW348, often taking Jeannie or Freddy with them. Wherever they went they drew admiring groups of onlookers. Especially so when, at the invitation of Major Ollie Squires, they flew over to the Army Air Corps HQ at Middle Wallop as guests of the Corps for their annual Open Day and Air Display. Whilst there they were entertained for lunch in the Officer's Mess. Here they were introduced to Major Squires Commanding Officer and senior members of the Royal Air Force whose duties encompassed liaison with the airborne troops. These dignitaries were greatly impressed by the work that Valentine and Giles had put into presenting TW348 as a pristine example of a wartime Air Observation Post machine. At some stage of the conversation, it was suggested that they should seek permission from the Board of Trade to demonstrate the capabilities of the Auster, and act as an ambassador for the wartime AOP Squadrons. Valentine was a little unsure at first but warmed to the idea, especially when it was suggested that both the Army and the

Air Force would support them in any way possible. The Army Air Corps' Commanding Officer went far as to offer training in AOP manoeuvres, and to sign Valentine off as a qualified military display Pilot. The only catch was that he would have to be a Commissioned Officer in the Territorial Army. Nothing was decided at that time. Valentine and Giles discussed the proposition in detail during the flight home, and later in the Old White Hart that evening. Valentine remained unsure about the commitment required to train as a Territorial Officer and Army Display Pilot balancing his internal arguments against his academic goals and future career. He discussed that matter with Jane and Jeannie, both of whom thought it was an opportunity too good to be true.

Still undecided, but warming to the idea, he took his dilemma to his tutor at Cranfield University. "Valentine," he said after staring out of his office window for several minutes, obviously deep in thought, "I don't see any reason why you should not combine your academic aspirations with those being handed to you on a plate by the Army Air Corps," he paused for a further minute or so and then continued, " I really do believe that here is a situation in which all parties will benefit. The University has good links with the Royal Air Force and some of the most important aircraft manufacturers; but we have very little contact with the airborne forces. You taking up a commission in the Army Air Corps whilst still pursuing your career objectives within the University would be of considerable benefit. Also," here he paused again before saying with a little chuckle "you would be silly to turn down flying a very interesting range of aircraft at the Queen's expense and being paid so to do. What say you now?"

Valentine looked really relieved and then smiling he asked, "may I use your 'phone sir?" Of course, my boy, feel free" was the swift response.

Valentine strode across the office and picked up the receiver: when the operator answered he said, "would you connect me to the Army Air Corps HQ at Middle Wallop please?" The phone was quickly answered by a voice with a north country brogue announcing, "Middle Wollup 'Ay Ay Sea Haitch Queue,' do yer naw the hextension numburr yer need?" "No, I'm sorry I don't. Could you connect me to Major Squires if he is available, please?" replied Valentine. After a short pause another voice spoke out "Major Squires telephone, can I be of assistance?" Valentine responded, "yes, I'm sure you can. Is the Major available please?" "He's just popped out along the corridor he'll be back in a jiffy. Would you care to hold?" Yes please," replied Valentine, "when he returns would you say that Valentine Shooter is on the line for him?" "Yes sir. Mr Shooter, are you any relation to a Captain Shooter who was lost in Normandy?" "Yes, my father" replied Valentine a little sharply. "I'm sorry sir, it's just that Captain Shooter is a bit of legend in the Corps, and I couldn't help but ask, I'm sorry for your loss sir. Oh! Here's the Major now." An abrupt "Squires" came down the line, "Hello uncle, Val here. I've thought through the proposition that I take a commission in the 'Terriers' to be trained as an Army Display Pilot. Everyone thinks that I'd be a fool not to follow up on it. What do we need to do now to get the ball rolling?" Ollie was overjoyed and said so in very direct terms, "I'll get the bumph moving from this end" he said, It won't take long to have you up for a pretty informal interview with a view to commissioning you as a Second Lieutenant in the 'Terriers'. Attestation will follow on pretty damn quick and then we will set about training you as an Officer, Gentleman, and as an Army Pilot. I am so pleased that you made the wise decision. Got to go now, tootle pip." With that he rang off.

Chapter 16

Celebrations

Several local, and more distant, flights were made so that Valentine and Giles could become thoroughly at home in the cockpit, and to learn the little foibles that all aircraft have in waiting to catch out the unwary or inattentive Pilot. On each flight he sensed, but was not distracted by, the presence of his father moulding him into a first-class Pilot with exceptional handling skills. Fuel consumption figures using a variety of throttle and mixture settings in a variety of different situations, and at different altitudes were compiled in order to plan their flights with, and without, fuel reserves. All were calculated for different load factors and weather conditions. During these flights Valentine had taken on the mantle of his father in that he insisted that Giles be taught how to manage the fuel, operate the radio and most importantly handle the Auster from the right-hand seat should Valentine become ill or otherwise incapacitated. Giles was a natural Pilot, probably due to his innate sympathy with anything mechanical: he resolved to undertake formal instruction to gain a private Pilot's Licence once their D-Day adventure was over.

June the sixth nineteen sixty-nine was now days away, all the necessary and sufficient planning the trip had been completed. The paperwork had been double checked, the planned route and possible diversions were marked on the aeronautical charts. Radio frequencies were listed, and the International Flight Plan had been filled out but not yet filed. All that was left to do was to get the meteorological reports for the planned flight, calculate the required headings to be flown adjusted for the winds aloft and to determine the time that would be taken on each leg of the plan between waypoints. Finally, they weighed their personal kitbags so that the weight and balance calculations could be made to ensure that the aircraft would be neither overloaded nor, so badly loaded that the natural stability of the aircraft would be compromised.

On the morning of the fifth of June there was air of excitement on the apron of Manor Farm's private airstrip due to the nature of the adventure to hand. The Flight Plan for an overseas flight would be filed with Air Traffic Control at Shoreham a couple of hours before their expected departure time and they planned to clear Customs at Shoreham Airport whilst they waited for the acknowledgement and acceptance of the flight plan. Whilst there the fifteen imperial gallon fuel tank was to be filled to the maximum that it would hold.

Jasper, Jane and Jeannie were ready to set off in Giles's Landrover to catch the mid-morning 'Sealink' ferry from Portsmouth to Ouistreham. The Landrover was not the most comfortable vehicle, but it was the only one available with enough space for the trio and their luggage, plus Giles's tool kit and maintenance spares for the Auster. They planned to drive into Caen where they hoped to catch up with the 'boys' before moving onto Bayeaux where they had rooms reserved from the fifth to the seventh of June in a small family run 'Pension' on the outskirts of Bayeaux.

The weather was gentle, and skies were clear, and the departure from Shoreham had gone without a hitch. They climbed to four thousand feet to cross the English Channel. At the midpoint of their track across the water they reported their position to the Controller working on the London Information airspace desk. He advised them to contact his French counterpart working the Lille Information desk. They had no difficulty in contacting the French airspace Controller who accepted them into French airspace and asked them to report when crossing the French coast. Once over the coast he provided them with information relevant to their arrival procedure into the Caen Airport Control Area. He instructed them to report their position when approaching the Visual Reporting Point designated 'November' for their descent to land at Caen. Their contact with the French air traffic people had been excellent, the Controllers being patient with them as they struggled with accented English and unfamiliar procedures. Their flight plan had worked out almost to the minute requiring a small revision to their estimated time of arrival at reporting point 'November' in readiness to receive their landing clearance for Caen. Nonetheless, the euphoria was tinged with relief after touching down at Caen's Carpiquet airport and taxying over to the airport arrivals apron.

The trip had been 'a piece of cake.' A couple of local Pilots who were involved in the organisation of the flying event for the celebrations called out "voici les aviateurs Anglais, tres brave." Then greeting them with rather formal hugs with kisses on both cheeks. Once they had collected their personal and the aircraft's documentation they were taken to 'book in' and complete their international arrival obligations. On presenting themselves in front of the Customs Officer Giles introduced a moment of deadpan comedy. The Douanier smiled a greeting whilst extending his right hand, "Bonjour Messieurs, vos passports s'il vous plait." Valentine dug into the left breast pocket of his flying overalls and produced his: Giles looked perplexed and said, "Passport! Passport! I've got my old army paybook, that's all I had last time I came here." The Douanier looked momentarily surprised and then worried, "Vous n'avez pas un passport monsieur?" Giles face broke into a grin, and he laughed "OK, mais oui" and from behind his back he produced his brand-new passport. "eh voila." The relief on the faces of all who were in the small office was a picture which had everybody laughing with Giles at his little joke. Giles got the first stamp in his passport; he offered the aircraft documents, the Douanier looked seriously the wallet being offered to him. "Un avion de guerre, n'est pas? Vous avez les mitrailleuses ou les bombes?" He looked sternly at Giles and Val and back again at the document wallet before grinning and waving them away, honour satisfied. After the humorous and friendly customs clearance, and the perfunctory check of their personal and aircraft documents, their new-found friends took them to the airport control office where the formalities of registering their arrival in France were completed.

The two host Pilots then took their charges back to their aircraft to collect their personal luggage and valuables before going through a small security gate in the perimeter fence. They then led them to a little car into which they, and their bags, were squashed for a short drive to a gate on the far side of the Airport which had a sign welcoming visitors to L'aeroclub de Caen. They piled out of the car and were ushered into the clubhouse where they met up with more locals and earlier international arrivals. The group was ushered into a wonderful restaurant which looked out over the Airport such that the comings and goings could be watched whilst meeting with the organisers of the event. A magnificent lunch was produced that comprised five courses of wonderfully prepared and presented food. Lunch, including several glasses of wine and spirits, was concluded at close to four in the afternoon.

They were whisked away along with other British arrivals in a tour coach to a YMCA near Bayeaux where they were to be accommodated for the duration of 'Les Celebrations.' They were more than ready to change out of their flying gear, and soak in a warm bath before making their way to the small private 'Pension' in which Jasper, Jane and Jeannie were staying. Val telephoned ahead to the 'Pension' to make the arrangements for the evening. Once the families were reunited, they took a taxi into the centre of the city where they would explore, take in the historic atmosphere of the town, and enjoy each other's company over a light evening meal. During their exploration of the town Val and Jeannie had walked hand-in-hand dawdling behind the others, they talked about all that they had enjoyed over the past year being together working on the Auster project and recognising their feelings for each other they started to plan for a future together. With dinner over Val said to everyone "Jeannie and I have been talking about the future. I am now going to ask her if she will be my wife." With smiles on all their faces and a round of applause that brought the other diners' attention onto their table Jeannie responded demurely "Val, I thought that you would never ask, of course I'll marry you!" Val then looked a little sheepish "I haven't bought you a ring yet, but we'll go and chose one as soon as we can. You've made me the happiest a man can be." Jane was overjoyed and told Jeannie that they must have a 'girls day out' to celebrate and start planning for the wedding. Giles finally managed to break into the chatter around the table to order a bottle of champagne so that he could propose a toast to the betrothed couple. A very happy party reluctantly broke up late that night when Giles and Val had to return to the YMCA and their beds; tomorrow would be another demanding day.

Despite the previously busy day they were both awake and up early looking to take a leisurely petit dejeuner of croissants, eggs, cheeses, a variety of cold meats and Café au Lait or hot chocolate served in massive cups. Their hosts had made arrangements for them to be taken back to Carpiquet shortly after ten where they were given a formal welcome and received a briefing about the events planned for the coming days. A specific briefing was given by a Senior Air Traffic Controller from Paris regarding the procedures which were to be followed. The different groups of aircraft that would be participating flew at a wide range of speeds so to present them in complete safety they were to fly past the VIP saluting base at Arromanches in an orderly stream. The Pilots of each group of aircraft were instructed form loose formations, or 'Balbos.' The slowest 'Balbo,' which would include the AOP aircraft, was to form up en route to Saint-Mere-l'eglise. From there the route was east to Utah beach and out to a point approximately half a mile offshore before turning right to follow the coast along the length of the remaining invasion beaches to the site of the Merville battery close to Ouistreham. From there the planned flight path would lead them a short distance inland to Pegasus Bridge at Ranville before taking a direct course to land at a specially prepared landing ground sited between the villages of Martragny and Vaux-sur-Seulles. Twenty-five years previously that field had been designated ALG B7.

They had just enough time to refuel and carry out their pre-flight checks on their aircraft before getting airborne and forming up in the pre-planned formation in readiness for the flypast as briefed.

The slowest aircraft participating were the AOP and Liaison contingent which included ten Austers of different Marks, seven Piper L-4 Grasshoppers, two Stinson L-5 Sentinels, and a lone Aeronca L-3 Grasshopper. As they progressed along the beaches to a point approximately two miles west of the VIP saluting base, they were overtaken by a heavier and faster group of warplanes which comprised a B25 Mitchell bomber, a B17 Flying Fortress, a Bristol Blenheim, a de Havilland Mosquito, a flight of Douglas DC3 Dakotas which would later be used as drop planes for a paratroop display, and the only airworthy Avro Lancaster which had been retained in RAF service; the last of this group to flypast the saluting base were the a fighters comprising half a dozen Spitfires, a lone Hurricane, and a flight of P51 Mustangs in missing man formation.

The AOP aircraft headed for the temporarily reactivated ALG B7 where they landed and were directed to park along a temporary fence line. Behind the fence lay a group of tents laid out in a similar pattern to that would have been used when the field was alive with invasion aircraft. A large khaki coloured marquee, which was in fact a former 'Bessoneau' hanger, had been erected close to the airstrip. This was the Operations Base for the re-activated ALG. Those Pilots whose aircraft were too valuable, or otherwise unsuited, to make a safe landing on a makeshift landing ground were instructed to land at Caen - Carpiquet, from whence they would be collected and taken by bus to ALG B7.

The Pilots found that their hosts had prepared a buffet lunch which comprised enormous piles of local fare and gallons of local wines, fruit juices and water. Before going to eat Val and Giles walked up and down the fence line that separated the landing strip from the public area looking for their family members with whom they spent the rest of the afternoon. The lunch was a leisurely affair and the aircrews who had participated in the flypast were finally returned to the YMCA in the late afternoon. They were warned to be ready to participate in a formal dinner that would he held at La Marie in Vaux-sur-Seulles; the tour coach would depart at seven thirty prompt. Jane, Jeannie and Jasper felt that it would not be 'the done thing' to gate crash the evening's entertainment. They decided to take themselves off to spend a quiet evening enjoying the sights and cafes in Caen.

That evening was one to be remembered, although there were quite a few participants who could remember very little of the event on the following morning, if ever. The Mayor welcomed the visiting airmen saluting them for their dedication in bringing their magnificent flying machines to their humble landing ground and then saluting the bravery of those who had come to their shores, their towns and villages to liberate 'La Belle France.' The Deputy Mayor of Bayeaux also added his greetings and salutations, as did the Chairman of the organising committee. Finally, the dinner was served, a small affair of only four courses, but a veritable feast that was enjoyed by all there. Then the Mayor again rose to propose the first of many toasts, too many for Giles who could 'hold his drink' but was starting to feel the effects of the wines and finally the Calvados. Amid much back slapping and protestations of enduring friendship the party broke up shortly after midnight. Upon returning to their accommodation Giles flopped down on his bed and said to Valentine, with whom he was sharing a room, "much more of this and we will be over our take-off weight limit." With that statement he fell asleep still partially dressed.

As before, their hosts had the transport organised and they were reunited with their aircraft shortly before lunch. The organisers had arranged for a small airshow to be held at the former ALG.

There were almost no professional display rated Pilots amongst the visitors and those who were, together with the Private Pilots who had volunteered to display their aircraft, had been briefed in Caen on the previous morning. Those who were not too hung over from the previous evening's revelry, and had agreed to participate, were taken aside into the Airfield Operations tent for an in-depth briefing regarding the safety arrangements applicable at the temporary airfield and the emergency procedures to be followed. With Gallic 'joi-de-vivre' and an attitude of 'rules are for the obedience of fools and the guidance of wise men' the Pilots were granted verbal display authority exemptions for this show only. The Air Traffic Controller from Paris was most insistent that no Pilot was to fly any part of his display routine at less than five hundred feet above the airfield. Valentine and several others were quite vociferous in pleading their case that the AOP aircraft operated at very low levels when in action and that the displays would lack realism unless they flew down to two hundred feet or less. The Controller was adamant that five hundred feet was an absolute minimum permitted by the aviation authorities and there would be serious repercussions if that limit was violated. He looked at the Pilots with a very stern expression as he said, "I will give you the altimeter pressure setting, and you will fly at not less than five hundred feet on that setting." He paused wagging the index finger on his right hand at each of them, "is that clearly understood?" Reluctantly, they all agreed with a sigh and a dejected "oui monsieur, entendu."

The time for take-off came round, the participating aircraft were individually cleared in turn to depart the airstrip. They were then to enter a holding pattern at one thousand five hundred feet above sea level a few miles away to the northwest. The official display was timed to start at two pm local time. The Air Traffic Controller called in a Spitfire that had just become airborne at Caen for a fast and low pass along the centre line of the airstrip. The Controller called up the Spitfire Pilot and passed the following instruction "you are to pass along the centre line of the airstrip at a height of not less than five hundred feet, the altimeter pressure setting is 'wan zayro wan sex' hectopascals. You are cleared to make fooer passes as briefed, the last will be in landing configuration before making a missed approach to return to Carpiquet" The Spitfire Pilot acknowledged and repeated back "not below five hundred feet, wun zero wun six on the altimeter, Spitfire, out." A few moments later the radio call "Spitfire inbound for high-speed pass" was heard on the radio. The Spitfire completed high speed then low speed passes followed by a running break with a barrel roll before flying a circuit as if to land. The Pilot flew a missed approach and the Pilot called "Spitfire departing to Caen." The Controller then called in a P51 Mustang to present a similar display. Again, the Pilot was given the altimeter setting for the airstrip.

Once the Mustang had cleared the area Valentine was called in to perform his short routine with his Air Observation Post Auster. The Controller again emphasised the altimeter setting as he cleared Val into the display box. His first pass was at cruising speed in straight and level flight with the altimeter rock steady at one thousand feet as if in transit to a shoot, upon reaching the far end of the field Val applied full power and pulled TW348 into an impossibly tight turn, standing the aircraft on her wingtip, then rolling wings level and slowing whilst descending to make a pass, downwind, along the far side of the field from the spectators. He pulled the aircraft round in another tight turn to align the aircraft down the centre line of the airfield. With two stages of flap set he very carefully flew the length of the runway at exactly five hundred feet at an airspeed, just above the stalling speed, of thirty-five miles per hour. The spectators watched in amazement and said that they felt they could have run faster. At the upwind end of the runway Valentine accelerated the little aircraft before initiating a climbing spiral to one thousand feet. Upon reaching that height over the field he called over the radio, "Auster display complete, downwind to land."

As he made his final turn to land back at the airstrip Valentine completed his pre-landing checks: these included the altimeter setting for the strip of one zero one six as given by the Air Traffic Controller. He expected to be at two hundred feet above the perimeter hedge at this point. However, the instrument was showing five hundred. He was committed to land, and continued visually only glancing at the airspeed indicator to ensure that his approach was stable and safe, without again referring to the altimeter. He made a perfect three-point landing. Then with the engine idling the aircraft rolled smoothly into its designated parking place. He applied the handbrake and shut down the engine by pulling the mixture control knob back to the 'idle cut-off' position, turned off the magnetos, fuel, the radio, and the master switch. He then checked the altimeter thinking that he must have mis-set it and expecting to be torn to shreds by an irate Controller. The instrument was correctly set but the height it showed was three hundred feet above that of the ground upon which he stood. Giles joined him as he, laughing almost uncontrollably, climbed out of the cockpit. "That wily old beggar of a Controller" he spluttered. "Threatened us with the possibility of a stay in the Bastille if we bust the five hundred feet above ground level as very sternly briefed. We were pretty peeved about it weren't we?" Giles agreed wondering what had got into his pal. "Just look at the altimeter, according to that we are three hundred feet above ground!" Giles guffawed "typical French under-handiness, he deserves the best bottle of the local 'plonk' we can find for him." For the rest of the afternoon the two men enjoyed the display in the company of their family members and other visiting aircrew, all of whom were very complimentary about Val's performance. They also spent time conversing, as best they could, with the local populace who had turned out en-masse to watch the free air-display. As before there was a buffet lunch for all who wanted one, some couldn't face the thought of yet more food after the wining and dining of the previous two days!

That evening they were left to their own devices. The boys, as Jane had started to call them, took a short quiet spell in their room. Both found themselves napping before freshening up and changing into their smart casual clothes. They then went down to the reception desk to order a taxi to take them into Bayeaux for a stroll around the town with their family members where they took in the historic atmosphere of the place. They took a table at an attractive bistro where they enjoyed a light meal and a bottle of wine between them.

Chapter 17

Deja Vu, again!

Jasper and the 'boys' stayed on in the Pension in Bayeaux for several days after the celebrations were over. Jane and Jeannie took the train and ferry home the following morning. Giles had made arrangements with his former REME comrades to meet up during the celebrations but the schedules for the aviators and the land-based contingents had not quite worked out too well and Giles felt that he had missed out a little. Nevertheless, some of his old chums had also decided to stay on in Normandy for a few extra days of visits to places that held special memories for them and reunions in in bars, cafes, restaurants and at the Commonwealth War Graves Cemeteries all of which made up for his earlier disappointment.

Jasper had left instructions with the farmhands to make hay whilst the sun was shining and to get it into storage for winter feed. Nevertheless, he felt a bit uncomfortable and told 'the boys' that he felt that he was being 'a bit of a shirker.' They used the Landrover so that they could visit the sites of the Battle for Normandy, the Commonwealth War Graves Cemeteries, the 'Musee de debarquement' in Bayeaux and the remains of the Mulberry harbour at Arromanches where Giles had disembarked in nineteen forty-four. Giles told Valentine of the various actions in which the Eleventh Armoured Division had been involved and recounted tales of his time there in the Battle for Normandy. At times Giles was quiet, reflective, occasionally almost morose, but in the main he was cheerful and shared the best and happiest of his memories. They walked on the Invasion Beaches and viewed the defensive gun emplacements along the coast. They visited the famous Gondree cafe at "Pegasus Bridge" and then moved onto the fields and villages in which 'Operation Goodwood' had been fought. The death ride of the Armoured Divisions is how one historian had later described that battle. Finally, a trip that followed the line of advance made by the Eleventh Armoured Division in 'Operation Bluecoat' from Balleroy to Vire and then swinging east-south eastwards towards Flers, from where the Division had started the closure of the base of the Falaise Pocket. A long and emotional stop was made at the Commonwealth War Graves Commission cemetery at St Charles de Percy between Le Beny Bocage and Vire for it was close to that spot where Alex had been hit and fatally wounded twenty-five years previously.

Jasper returned to England that evening on the night ferry from Ouistreham to Portsmouth. He had the Landrover loaded with the luggage that 'the boys' would no longer need for their last night in Bayeaux. Valentine and Giles planned on making a last flight over the battlefields of 'Operation Bluecoat' on the following afternoon. They reckoned that the whole morning would be taken up with checking out of the Pension in Bayeaux, getting themselves to the Airport at Carpiquet and completing the legal requirements for their return flight to England which would include their final battlefield tour. It was agreed that Valentine and Giles would contact their respective parents giving them an approximate time of arrival in Goodwood where they planned to clear Customs. They would then refuel before making the short 'hop' home to Upham Manor.

They gathered the meteorological information for the Region and for the Southern Coastal Area of England in order to create their Flight Plan. The weather had been changeable when they left England on their great adventure to Normandy. They were relieved to find that a strong area of high pressure had established in the North Sea giving light and variable southerly winds to carry them home across the Channel. "That's a good omen," said Valentine. "A light southerly breeze was called an 'Auster' by the Romans in antiquity and we shall have an 'Auster' carrying our Auster home."

They completed their planning: the weight and balance calculations showed that with their personal kit plus a full tank of fuel that they were within the legal limits for the flight. Flying at a gentle cruising speed of ninety miles per hour they would have sufficient fuel for their aerial tour that would pass over the places associated with 'Operation Bluecoat' before setting course for home. They completed their legal obligations for their departure from France and were given permission to activate their cross-channel Flight Plan whilst airborne once they had completed their flight inland to the area around Vire. The fuel tank was filled to the top and they departed from Caen heading south-west towards Vire. Their planned route was to turn overhead the town of Vire en route to Flers before heading slightly west of north to cross the French coast near Courseulles – sur – Mer where they would call the Controller at Lille Information to activate their International Flight Plan.

They overflew, and took photographs of, the ALG from which Alex Shooter and his observer had so hastily departed on that fateful day in nineteen forty-four; a field to which they would never return. Alex and Bill had been tasked with registering the guns of the of Eleventh Armoured Divisional Artillery onto enemy forces which were advancing along the line of, and across, the highway from Vire to Le Beny Bocage. The German armoured thrust was directly threatening the left flank of the Division's spearhead. As Val and Giles approached the village of St Charles de Percy the skies seemed take on a different hue, a deeper bluish grey in the clouds that had formed to cover most of the skies around them; and there was a deep mistiness developing in the valley of the Souleuvre river below them. They spotted smoky fires in the landscape ahead and a little to the left of their track. The landscape appeared, ostensibly, to be the same: but strangely different, the main road leading to Vire suddenly seemed narrower. The traffic on it was kicking up small dusty trails. Feeling confused and slightly worried Val asked Giles "have we just flown into a film set for a war movie?" Giles was the first to react when he spotted a World War two Armoured Recovery Vehicle idling at the entrance to a green lane on the southern slope of the valley. They soon realised that the traffic comprised military lorries, scout cars and armour: all with white star recognition signs painted on their bonnets and roofs. "What the blazes, what's happening!" they shouted almost in unison. Giles having less to do than Valentine who was concentrating on his flying yelled "where the hell are we?" After a pause he spoke more quietly "perhaps that should be when, the hell are we?" The air suddenly filled with a sound like swarm of angry bees passing close by their ears, occasional 'wumph' sounds and deeper toned 'swooshing' noises assailed their senses, they realised that these were the sounds of battle, and that they were well and truly in the midst of it.

Valentine pulled the stick back and hard over into his right groin at the same time he plunged the throttle knob fully forward into the panel. The Auster stood on her starboard wing tip making a climbing turn to the right, once heading north again and away from the horror of that which they had just experienced the wings were levelled. A dazed Valentine relaxed the back pressure on the stick whilst simultaneously pulling back the throttle knob until the engine was running at cruising revs. He then re-trimmed her to fly at ninety miles per hour in a gentle climb. They looked at each other and then at their surroundings; Valentine said thoughtfully "I think that we have encountered a time warp." Giles nodded his agreement, his mind was in a turmoil, his thoughts were "how can I have been caught in a time warp that has placed me in a time that I have previously experienced?" Both the men, in their different worlds, were carried along by the reliable and stable little aircraft that they had done so much to bring back into service. Giles started to understand that it was the aircraft that had jumped through time, and his physical body was still in the present, Valentine was lost in a dreamlike state with his hands and feet responding to the air currents that would otherwise have caused the aircraft to deviate from its course.

Their 'nightmare' was far from over: the weather was closing in, and the radio was dead. There were few ground references visible as the mist that had started to form in the valleys earlier had become a blanket of pale grey draped over the land. The sky had become ominously overcast and darkening, but the air remained strangely calm as the little Auster droned on, gradually gaining height and holding her northly course. The two men were now in worlds of their own, lost in thought: fighting both flashbacks and images from recited stories which were deeply embedded in their respective minds. Valentine vaguely had the sense that once again he was flying with his dad in control of their aircraft.

Meanwhile, the stable little Auster had crossed the French coast in a gentle climb and was maintaining a steady course slightly east of north. The Air Traffic Control Oficer at Caen had tried several times to contact G-UNNR without success. He had contacted his counterpart at Lille Information who dealt with cross-channel traffic. The Controller in Lille tried, unsuccessfully, to make contact with the crew of Auster that was now nearing mid-channel and the International Boundary between the Paris and London Air Traffic Control Regions. The radar plot of an unresponsive aircraft believed to be G-UNNR was passed over to the Controller on the London Information Desk. The British Controller similarly failed to establish radio contact with the unknown traffic now entering British Airspace. London Control requested an Air Sea Rescue helicopter to be deployed from RAF Tangmere to intercept the silent inbound aircraft.

After a time Valentine, who could not recall how long if he ever really knew, recovered his sense of the 'here and now' and instinctively completed his en-route cockpit checks. The fuel-gauge was showing a whisker over three gallons, barely enough for another half an hour of powered flight. That equated to roughly forty nautical miles in the gentle southerly wind before she would become a glider: one with a fairly steep glide angle. The clouds were now much less foreboding, being higher and lighter in colour, there were breaks in places through which shafts of sunlight were blazing. He sensed, rather than saw, a Westland Whirlwind Air Sea Rescue helicopter moving into loose formation with him off his port wing. In the hazy light he saw a coastline which formed a triangular promontory far below, a little to the right of the aircraft's nose, some ten miles ahead of them. 'Selsey Bill' popped into Valentine's fuddled mind. The helicopter Pilot was waving as if to get Valentine's attention, but he was too mentally lost and physically drained to respond. The helicopter Pilot then gestured pointing down, and then straight ahead. Again, Valentine could not comprehend the signals and sank once more into a semi-comatose state with his mind in torment.

He was jerked back to reality, startled and confused, as the engine began coughing and spluttering. It picked up again, only to cough twice more before dying completely. Val looked around and muttered, "where the blazes are we now?" The atmosphere was still quite heavy with a partially overcast sky through which rays of sunshine provided patchily illuminated ground features which were hard to identify. Giles, also jerked out of his unresponsive state by the unfamiliar noises from the engine slowly responded, "I'm not completely sure but I think that might be Middle Down to our left." The propeller was windmilling, worse than useless, as it was being driven by the relative airflow. The airspeed bled away. With zero thrust from the engine, and the additional drag from the windmilling propellor, the nose of the aircraft dropped further below the horizon. She descended slowly at first, but the rate of descent started to increase as gravity took over from thrust and accelerated the machine. As the airspeed rose the aerodynamic forces once more balanced out, with the greater airspeed the lift generated by the wings increased and the nose of the aircraft started come up towards the horizon; this porpoising effect was quickly damped out and the indicated airspeed settled once more to the ninety miles per hour for which the aircraft had been trimmed whilst fleeing from the Battlefield over Normandy. Val quite automatically reached up for the trimming handle and moved it forward with his right hand whilst applying a little back pressure to the stick to slow the little aircraft to an indicated airspeed of fifty miles per hour to obtain the optimum glide angle.

Sunlight breaking through the high overcast gave Val and Giles a clear view of the ground ahead which rapidly became more recognisable. Val saw the far end of a runway made of pierced steel planks aligned almost south to north. The grass, which had grown thorough the planking, had been mown to delineate the runway. Off to the right was the wartime Watch Office and the other aerodrome buildings. He knew their faithful Auster had done it again; it had brought its crew home.

G-UNNR cleared a stand of trees surrounding a group of dilapidated huts, gliding comfortably above a country lane and the boundary hedge before it skimmed across the concrete track which connected the lane to the runway and the paved perimeter tracks. On the perimeter track to the right of the runway a group of vehicles was parked; the occupants were waiting for arrival of Val and Giles returning from France. The vehicles tore off along the track to swing onto the runway in pursuit of the aircraft. The Air Sea Rescue helicopter had followed the Auster down and landed on the apron in front of the hanger. The winchman jumped out carrying his first aid bag and ran over to the edge of the runway waving to the Driver of the Jeep which was already moving toward the runway in order to follow the aircraft. Jasper was at the wheel of his faithful old Jeep; he pulled over to pick up the winchman before setting again in pursuit of the Auster. Jane, together with Jeannie in her sports tourer, raced on to pass the Jeep. They were followed by Giles' wife with Old Bill and Freddy in the Land Rover.

Valentine was aware that he should be raising the nose of the Auster to bring it into the three-point attitude for landing, but for some reason he could not make his arms respond or find the strength. As if responding to his will the aircraft levelled out in the ground effect. She sank towards the ground, not quite in the three-point attitude, the main wheels touched the runway. She bounced, and settled again, this time slightly tailwheel first which pitched her onto her main wheels. That caused another small bounce before the aircraft finally settled onto all three wheels. Mercifully, the wind had dropped away to nothing, and she rolled along the runway in a straight line. Eventually she came to a stand near the northern end of the runway. TW348 had returned home, just as she had twenty-five years previously.

Both Giles and Valentine sat there shocked and bemused. Jasper's Willys Jeep screeched to a halt beside aircraft, the Land Rover drawn up on the other side, and Jane's tourer was slewed round in front of the aircraft, as much as to say, "you've gone far enough!" Strong hands freed the safety harnesses from the unresponsive Pilot and his chum. Jasper, Jane, Jeannie and the others were startled to find 'the boys' looking extremely shocked and drained of energy. Valentine was gently lifted from the cockpit and set on the ground with his back supported against the port main wheel, Giles was lifted out of the starboard side and wrapped in a blanket as he sat down rather quickly, as if drunk, on the starboard wheel. Both men were conscious, but drained of colour, seeming mentally detached and unaware of what was happening around them. Jasper said to Giles "you look like you've seen a ghost son." "I have" Giles replied, "I have." On the other side of the aircraft Jane was leaning over her son with her soon to be daughter-in-law who was gently embracing her fiancée. Tears were streaming down their faces when Val whispered to them, with a wistful smile on his lips, "I'm afraid I'm a little late for dinner."

<end>

Author's Postscript

In late nineteen ninety-three members of the then named International Auster Pilot Club received an invitation from the Organisers of an event that was to be held as part of the Fiftieth anniversary of D-Day. The Organizing Committee were principally aircraft owners and Pilots based in Caen. They had secured permission to reopen a former Advanced Landing Ground (ALG B7) close to the small town of Vaux-sur-Seulles near Bayeaux as the focal point for the planned celebrations which would take place over a period of several days. The townspeople were very supportive of the idea and the celebrations included a reception and dinner in the town hall. The author and Alan Buckley, his partner in aviation adventures, were accompanied by the author's youngest son Jonathan, to take part in these celebrations. They were flying their Auster Mark V alpha, a civilianised AOP Mark V. The event included a formation fly-past of the invasion beaches by all the visiting aircraft, and a carefully planned but informal flying display by some of the Pilots at ALG B7 before being entertained by their French hosts at a grand reception held in the town hall of Vaux-sur-Seuilles. In this event were laid the seeds of "From the mists of time."

The author, and his chum Alan Buckley, also participated in the Tiger Club's prestigious annual "Dawn to Dusk" flying competition in which competitors submit plans for a flight with a specific purpose, to be flown between the hours of dawn and dusk over the course of a single day. One such entry had the objective of following the movements of the Second Northamptonshire Yeomanry an Armoured Reconnaissance Regiment in the Royal Armoured Corps. The Author's father served in that Regiment during the Second World War. This task proved to be too much for completion in one day. Two separate entries, in different years, were planned and each were flown in a single day. The second competition entry was made in nineteen ninety-seven: it covered the Regiment's activities as the Reconnaissance Regiment of the Eleventh Armoured Division during invasion of Normandy, and subsequent actions following the retreating German army as they passed through northern France, into Belgium and Holland. Sadly, the Auster was not available for those flights due to the need for heavy maintenance which, in the event, became a complete rebuild. The research required for the Dawn to Dusk competition 'closed the loop' and from those experiences the concept of the story "From the mists of time" was revealed to the author.

Finally, the detail of the life of a Royal Artillery Officer serving with the British Expeditionary Force in France and Belgium in nineteen forty, and during the retreat to Dunkirk, was built upon the experiences of a Battery Officer, known simply as 'GunBuster', serving with a Field Artillery Regiment during that period.

www.ingramcontent.com/pod-product-compliance
Lightning Source LLC
Chambersburg PA
CBHW021159310726
48971CB00002B/703